The Chase

A Novel of the American Civil War

By

Blair Howard

ISBN-13: 978-1508981657

ISBN-10: 1508981655

Contents

The Chase

Chapter 1

March 30, 1865 - Elbow, Kansas

They rode into the small town of Elbow, Kansas, at a little after three o'clock on the afternoon of Thursday March 30, 1865. It was one of those bright and balmy spring days: blue skies, scudding white clouds, chilly with a light breeze.

There were twenty-three of them. A scruffy-looking bunch; slouched in their saddles, hair long and unkempt, unshaven. They rode slowly and silently eastward along the single street. Their gray uniforms, what was left of them, were soiled, threadbare, and washed out. It was barely possible to tell that they were Confederate soldiers.

They were led by a diminutive individual, a lieutenant. He was the better dressed of the group, but not by much. He sat low in the saddle, hunched over the pommel. His skin was weathered, the color of tanned hide. His features were sharp, heavily lined, accentuated by a small, pointed beard and a heavy mustache. His dark brown eyes were hooded below heavy brows, sunken, cold, and glittering. He wore his already graying hair long, to the shoulder; it was unkempt, hanging in greasy strands. His name was Jesse Quintana, and at the age of thirty-six, he was a legend, infamous, more bandit than soldier. From the earliest beginnings of the war, he had been one of William Quantrill's Confederate raiders, bushwhackers.

Quintana's small force included a sergeant, two corporals, and nineteen troopers. There was no military structure to the group, no order; they were a disorderly bunch that rode into town looking for trouble and whatever loot they could find.

Disorderly they might be, but Lieutenant Quintana was an able and wily battlefield commander, and he ruled his men with an iron hand. These were fearless, brutal men; they were all that was left of Bloody Bill Anderson's Regiment.

Anderson, the most feared of Quantrill's lieutenants was long dead, killed at Centralia in 1864. Upon his death, another legend, Arch Clement, had taken over the leadership of the guerrilla band and for more than a year they had roamed across Kansas and Missouri, killing and robbing Federal soldiers and civilian sympathizers alike. Clement was a master of guerilla warfare.

Quintana and Clement, however, did not like each other, and they were almost always at odds. Finally, after a falling out that left Clement wounded, Quintana and his ruffians broke away from the main group and set out upon a trail of mayhem and terror that stretched from Lexington, Missouri, to Elbow.

Quintana's soldiers, all of them, were veterans of the now famous Lawrence, Kansas, Massacre of August 21, 1863, when more than four hundred of Quantrill's raiders attacked the town, robbing most of the banks, looting the stores, and killing more than a hundred and eighty five unarmed men and boys. Now, they were in Elbow....

Elbow, located in the southeast corner of Kansas just four miles west of Fort Scott, was one of those tiny, wind-blown western settlements that seemed to be springing up, every dozen, or so, miles all across the state. It was no more than a collection of perhaps sixty wood-built dwellings, a small church, a one-room school house, a general store, and a saloon (if you could call it that), all set along either side of a single dusty street: population one hundred forty four.

Most of the townsfolk were employed at nearby Fort Scott, a large Federal military base and hospital. The fort also housed a large contingent of Federal cavalry and several regiments of infantry, but, for now at least, that was of little interest to Quintana. He and his men had been on the road for five days, they were tired, hungry and broke, and they were looking for some ... well, recreation.

Set midway along the street on the south side, the general store in Elbow was run by a young couple, Gabe and Bonnie Powell.

Bonnie was an Irish immigrant. She'd arrived in the United States as a small child, accompanied only by her father, who had long ago passed away, and her older brother, a Federal soldier away fighting in the war.

Bonnie, now twenty-five years old, was a tall young woman, almost five feet ten inches tall, slender, with dark brown hair that hung in ringlets to her shoulders. She was an attractive woman; not really beautiful, but ... well, she was pretty. She had a small oval face, large brown eyes, and a small mouth with lips that, to some, might be just a little too thin. She wore a pale yellow gingham dress tied at the waist with a dark blue ribbon.

Bonnie had met Gabe Powell at a dance at Fort Scott, where she was living at the time. It had been love at first sight, for both of them. They married three months later, and were soon settled into Gabe's small general store. Now, two years on, they were expecting their first child.

At the east end of the street, the small non-denominational church was run by Reverend Mica Jones and had been for more than twenty years. Now in his late sixties, Jones was the well-loved leader of the small population of Elbow.

Across the street from the church, in the tiny schoolhouse, the children of Elbow, all nine of them, were taking their daily lessons.

When the Confederates soldiers turned onto the street and entered Elbow from the west, Reverend Jones was out front of the church, sweeping the porch. He spotted them immediately and his blood ran cold, for he recognized them for exactly what they were.

Jones dropped his broom and ran inside the church. As he did so, Quintana, seeing him go, put spurs to horse and galloped toward the church.

Jones ran through the church, past the table that served as the altar, grabbed the bell rope, and hauled on it; the bell in the cupola above the church roof clanged loudly. As it did so, Jesse Quintana arrived at full gallop outside the front door and, even before the horse had slid to a stop, he was out of the saddle and running up the front steps and into the church, pulling a pistol from his belt as he ran.

The bell clanged again.

Without a word, and before the bell could sound for a third time, Quintana shot the Reverend Jones in the side of the head, killing him instantly.

Quintana stood over the dead man, his legs akimbo. The pistol, now at his side, was still smoking and hung loosely in his fingers, pointing down at the wooden floor. He spat into the blood that pooled out over the wood planks, then turned and walked quickly back out of the church and onto the street where his men were waiting for him, most of them still mounted.

"Jeb," he said to one of the still mounted troopers, "head east 'bout a half-mile along the road, find a good spot, an' keep a lookout. Y'see anythin' move, anythin' at all, you hightail it back heah fast as you can. Smith, you go west; same thing; keep a sharp lookout there. Sergeant Brown, you, Jack, Abe, Louis, Henry, you're with me. The rest of y'all," he shouted, "go an' round everyone up. Go house to house." He looked across the street at the schoolhouse, nodded his head in its direction and said, "Them too. Bring 'em all to the church an' shut 'em inside. Don't let anyone get away."

Quintana grabbed his horse's dangling reins, swung himself up into the saddle, pulled its head around and, followed by Brown and his four companions, headed slowly down the street toward the general store.

Bonnie Powell was not alone inside the store when she heard the bell; there was also a customer, a man of about fifty years of age, sorting through a box of tools just to the left of the counter where Bonnie was tending to the business of the day. Her husband, Gabe, was out back, a couple of hundred yards away across a pasture, inside the barn attending the needs of their two horses and four cows.

When they first heard the church bell, and then the single gunshot that had killed the Reverend Jones, Bonnie and her customer looked up from what they were doing and out through the storefront windows. They heard the sound of horses approaching the store and what Bonnie saw filled her with dread.

Quintana, followed by Sergeant Jedidiah Brown and the four troopers, stomped heavily into the store. Bonnie, wide-eyed with terror, backed away from the counter; her customer turned and pressed his back against the shelving.

Without saying a word, Quintana drew his pistol and shot the customer between the eyes. The man dropped heavily to floor—dead, killed instantly.

"Well now," Quintana said with a smirk as he holstered his still smoking gun, "what do we have heah?"

Bonnie was terrified. Unable to believe what had just happened, she stuttered, "You—you—you'd better get out of here." She placed her back to the shelving, both hands on the bump of her belly. "My husband is out back. I only have to call—"

"So call," Quintana said with a grin. "Everyone's welcome heah. Come one, come all, I say."

He looked round at the men gathered behind him, twitched his head in Bonnie's direction and, with a grin, said, "I gotta get me some o' that. Lock the door, Sergeant."

Brown did as he was asked.

"Now, little lady. Why don't you just step right around heah, so's we can get a good look at ya?"

She shook her head, and pressed her back firmly against the shelving at the rear of the counter.

"I said, step around heah ... NOW!"

Bonnie jumped as he shouted, and, with tears in her eyes, she did as she was told.

"Please, don't hurt me ... my baby," she whispered, looking down at her belly.

Quintana did not reply. He walked slowly around her, his spurs tinkling. He trailed the tips of his fingers across the front of her bodice, over her shoulder and down the small of her back to her buttocks. He squeezed the left one, nodded his head in appreciation, and

15

continued with his exploration, from the back around to the front. He ran the tips of his fingers over her belly, and she shuddered.

"Why don't you just slip outa that pretty dress, darlin'" Be a shame to tear it pullin' it off ya."

"Oh nooo, please," she burst into tears. "I'm pregnant. You'll hurt my baby."

"Yeh, pregnint. I like that. Ain't never had me a pregnint woman afore. This'll be the first time."

He pulled a large knife from a sheath at his waist.

"NOW, GET OUTA THAT DRESS, an' whatever doodads you might be a wearin' under it. I want to see you neckid."

Slowly, as the six men watched, all grinning widely, she did as she was told. She stood before them, naked and scared. Quintana nodded his head in appreciation.

She tried to cover herself with her hands but it was useless. The smile on Quintana's face disappeared, and was replaced by a look of grim determination.

"Take your han's away, Darlin'. Lemme see what ya got."

Resigned, she dropped her hands to her side, and whimpered as tears ran down her cheeks.

Quintana nodded his head again. He licked his lips lasciviously, and said, quietly to his men, "Grab her, boys. Take an arm and a leg each an' spread her. You 'old her 'ead, Sergeant. 'Old her tight, boys. Me first, then y'all can take turns."

16

It was then that Gabe Powell burst into the room from the rear of the store. He stopped dead, stared wide-eyed at his naked wife, and shouted, "NOOOOO."

"Well, hello there," Quintana said, drawing the revolver from the holster at his side, "an' goodbye."

He cocked the pistol, leveled it, and shot Powell in the face.

Bonnie screamed once, then fainted, and fell in a heap on the floor.

"Well, now. Ain't that a whole lot better?" Quintana said, undoing his belt and allowing his britches to fall around his boots.

Less than ten minutes later, they were finished—all of them—and Bonnie Powell lay, only half-conscious, on the floor in front of the sales counter. She was bruised and bleeding, her dead husband only feet away behind the counter, the dead customer another couple of feet away to her left.

"Y'all sort through this place," Quintana said, looking around. "Grab anythin' o' value, especially guns and ammo. There are three o' cases o' cartridges for the Henry over there, behind the counter. Them boxes hold twenny-five hundred rounds a piece. Drag 'em outside and share 'em among the men. Can't never have too many."

Quintana's men ransacked the store, taking what money there was in the register, and all the ammunition and guns they could carry.

Quintana was the last man to leave the store. He looked around once more after his men had left, and, seeing the heels of Gabe Powell's boots sticking out from behind the counter, he grinned. He walked around the end of the counter, pulled the knife from his belt as he went, and stooped over the dead man for a moment. He turned again, holding something in his left hand, and walked to the front door as he returned the knife to his belt.

He stopped at the open doorway, thought for a moment, then turned around and looked at Bonnie. He nodded his head, grinned, and calmly pulled his pistol from its holster and shot her in the chest.

Outside, the town was in shambles; the people, those they could find—about forty—including the teacher and children from the school, had been rounded up and were locked in the church. Inside, the smaller children were crying, one or two were even screaming. Houses had been ransacked, and everything of value had been gathered together, bundled, and then loaded onto the horses. Some of the men were stuffing food into their mouths, some were wearing fancy women's hats; all were laughing and joking.

"Fire it," Quintana said, mounting his horse and making ready to ride.

Sergeant Brown leaped onto the front porch of the church. He held a large can of coal oil, which had been taken from the store, and was followed closely by two men carrying flaming rags. He ran to the front door and poured the oil around the foundations of the wooden building.

It was at that moment that Jeb Fletcher, the lookout that Quintana had sent to watch the road to the east, came galloping, at full speed, back into town.

"We gotta get outa heah." he shouted. "Federal cavalry's a comin', a whole passel of 'em. They're about five minutes away and ridin' fast."

"Finish that, Sergeant," Quintana yelled at Brown. "An' be quick about it. You, men; light it up. Now, now, do it now."

Within seconds, the east end of the wooden building was in flames. The north wall and front door were ablaze, and inside the church, the trapped people were coughing and screaming.

"Let's go."

Quintana's men struggled to contain their panicky mounts, but soon were back in the saddle and headed out of Elbow at full gallop; into the open country to the west.

Less than five minutes later, the Federal troopers arrived at the burning church and could hear the screams coming from within.

"Round back," the Federal captain yelled. He leapt down from his horse, as it skidded to a stop. "There's a door round back. Break it down. Get 'em outa there."

The rest of the troop dismounted, leaving their horses to run free in the street. Six men ran to the rear of the church and, after several tries, managed to smash down the door and run inside; into clouds of billowing smoke and panicking people and children.

They herded the folk out into the open. Some of the older people had been overwhelmed by the smoke and had to be carried; all of them were choking, coughing, and spluttering. The church continued to burn.

"There's a pump in front of the store," someone shouted. "Get some buckets and form a chain. Get that fire out." But there were few buckets to be found, and in less than thirty minutes, the old church was reduced to a pile of blazing timbers.

"Did you get everyone out, Lieutenant?"

"I think we did, sir, but we'll not know for sure until we can figure out who was in there and who wasn't; it'll take a while, I guess."

"Captain."

"Yes, Corporal. What is it?"

"I think you'd better come an' look at what we found in the store, sir."

The captain, followed by the corporal, a sergeant, and the lieutenant, ran down the street and into the store.

"Oh God; oh Christ. Is she dead?"

"No sir, there's a pulse, an' a strong one. She just might make it."

"Cover her. Find a wagon. We need to get her to the hospital; quickly now, and be gentle as you can. That man over there is dead. What about the man behind the counter?"

Oh, he's daid, sir, an' scalped too."

Chapter 2

April 3rd, 1865 - Federal Headquarters, Nashville, TN

Captain Ignatius Ronan O'Sullivan was in his tent talking to Sergeant Boone Coffin when the messenger from Colonel Abel Streight found him.

"The colonel would like a word with you, Captain, as soon as you can, sir."

"Thank you, Lieutenant," O'Sullivan said, rising from the folding stool upon which he was sitting. "Any idea what he wants? No, of course you wouldn't. Tell Colonel Streight that I'll be there in just a minute."

The lieutenant nodded, saluted, spun on his heel, and walked quickly away.

"Well now, me old son," he said to Sergeant Boone Coffin," I wonder what that can be about." The two men had been sitting together, talking, and drinking coffee; theirs was an unusual friendship, and not one that was widely known of around the Federal Headquarters at Nashville, Tennessee.

"Better go see, I suppose," he said, reaching for his uniform coat. "Need to clean up a bit first, though. Can't let the old man see me all dusty, an' all."

Coffin looked up at him, grinned, and said, "Probably gonna promote you to major."

"Not likely, old son," O'Sullivan said, buckling the heavy leather belt. "I only got this promotion 'cause all

22

the others more qualified got 'emselves killed at Franklin. Bumped up from sergeant major to captain; that's bloody unheard of, that is. An' there's a lot of junior officers that didn't take it any too well, so there are."

O'Sullivan, born and raised in County Cork in Ireland, was a tall, heavy-set man: over six feet and two hundred and forty pounds of solid muscle. At forty-two years old, he was still in his prime: his black hair showed not a hint of gray.

He wore his hair long, just to the collar. His facial hair was limited to a huge mustache that swept away from his upper lip to join with even bigger sideburns—a style made famous by Federal Major General Burnside— his chin was clean-shaven. His eyes were deep blue, with tiny lines radiating away from the corners that gave him the look of a man who laughed a lot; which he did, it was part of his Irish make up. He was an impressive man, by any standards, and he had a demeanor to match. He stood, when he did stand, rigidly erect, his chest a great barrel, his arms knotted with muscles.

His brand new captain's uniform was indeed already clean, but still he took a small brush from his locker and went through the motions of sweeping away any imaginary specks of dust. That done, he straightened his jacket, adjusted the leather belt, took his kepi from on top of his footlocker and set it squarely on his head, flipped Coffin a mocking salute, and then ducked out through the flap of the tent and strode quickly away.

"There's been an incident in Elbow, Captain," Colonel Abel Streight said, without bothering to offer the niceties of a greeting, as he waved O'Sullivan to a chair set in front to his desk.

O'Sullivan looked sharply at him, worried.

"Incident, Colonel? What incident?"

"I don't have all the details, Captain. In fact, I know very little. What I do know arrived by telegraph from Fort Scott less than thirty minutes ago. It seems your sister is in hospital, and that her husband is dead. More than that, I cannot say.

"You'll want to leave for Kansas at once, I assume. You have my permission to do so, Captain. I have already filled out your leave of absence, and General Thomas has approved it. You'll note that it's open-ended, no time limit" Streight handed him the document, "so you'll not need to worry about returning quickly. You may leave as soon as you wish, but please make sure all is well with the 51st before you go. Here's the order transferring command of the regiment to Captain Scearcy. You'll need to handle that too, of course." He handed O'Sullivan the written order, then continued, "Oh, and take Sergeant Coffin with you. He will not be fit to live with, should you leave him here."

"Sir, I... I... I."

"Yes, I know, Captain. Please, do not worry. Take as much time as you need ... you've earned it, not just at Franklin, but time and again. No one, and I mean no one, was more pleased than I was when General Thomas confirmed your commission. It should have happened a long time ago.

"Fort Scott must be, what, all of two weeks ride from here, maybe more? Your regiment will be waiting for you when you return."

O'Sullivan's normally tanned face had gone white: his little sister, Bonnie... *What in God's name has happened?*

"Thank you, Colonel, sir. I'll be back just as soon as I can."

"Yes, yes," Streight replied brusquely. "But, take your time. This damnable war is about to end. We've done for Hood and his Army of Tennessee, and, so I'm told, General Lee has lost Petersburg, and Richmond, and is in retreat westward. Grant will, I have no doubt, finish him off, and quite quickly. Once Lee is done for, so too will be the rest of the Confederacy.

"Take care of yourself, Captain. I will be forever grateful for all you have done for me over the past several years, and especially so during our foray into Alabama. Go now. Go see to your sister. All will be well here."

"Thank you, sir. Thank you very much."

O'Sullivan, stood up, came rigidly to attention, saluted his brigade commander, and then turned and walked quickly out of the room. The minute the door closed behind him, he stopped, leaned back against the wall with his head in his hands, and tried to concentrate.

Oh, m'God. What the hell has happened? Bonnie in hospital, he thought in despair. *The baby? Gabe dead?* He pulled himself together. He had much to prepare and a long way to go.

"Start packin', Boone," O'Sullivan said as he ducked under the flap of the tent. "We're out o' here. We're going to Kansas."

"Kansas?" Coffin asked. "Why Kansas, for God's sake?"

"It's Bonnie. She's in hospital at Fort Scott, an' Gabe's dead. So start packin', you're comin' with me. I'll be back in a few minutes. I need to turn the regiment over to Scearcy. We leave as soon as we're packed." Then he turned and left the tent.

"Hey, wait a minute," Coffin shouted. "What the hell has happened? What about the baby?"

"I don't know. Lemme go sort things out with the regiment an' I'll be back, an' then we'll talk. Right now, I got too much on me mind."

He was back in less than an hour, his duty to the 51st completed, and command transferred to his junior captain. Coffin already had their clothes and personal items packed into two small paniers and two sets of saddle bags. O'Sullivan didn't bother to check them; he trusted Coffin implicitly.

"So tell me, for Christ's sake," Coffin said. "What the hell has happened?"

26

Sergeant Boone Coffin was a small man, just five feet eight inches tall, skinny to a fault—he weighed less than a hundred and thirty pounds. He was thirty years old, but other than knowing that, his origins were unknown, even to him. He wore his thin, receding hair long; shoulder length. His narrow face was deeply tanned, clean-shaven, and he was blessed with a pair of hooded, hazel eyes that missed nothing. His looks were deceptively mundane: he was an extremely intelligent man, resourceful, and a survivor par excellence, and he had no master other than Captain Ignatius O'Sullivan. And O'Sullivan had long ago recognized Coffin's worth, and took every advantage it; they had a truly reciprocal and symbiotic relationship.

"I don't know much; just that Gabe is dead an' Bonnie is in hospital at Fort Scott. The Old Man received a telegraph not much more'n a couple o' hours ago, an' that was about all it said. He must have moved on it pretty quick, 'cause he had our leaves of absence already written out and signed by General Thomas."

"How long we gonna be gone, Captain? Fort Scott's more'n five hundred miles away; that's fifteen, maybe twenty days hard ride."

"We ain't ridin'. We'll take a train to Kansas City an' then ride south from there. If all goes well, we should be at Fort Scott in less than a week. Leave that stuff here for now; let's go see to the animals."

The animals—O'Sullivan's horse, Lightning, and Coffin's mule, Phoebe—were both veterans of Colonel

Abel Streight's now famous raid into Northern Alabama. Both were stabled with the 13th Indiana Cavalry, about a half-mile away. The two animals had, over the two years they had been together, become close friends; now, they stood together, their heads over the split rail fence, watching the rest of the cavalry horses being put through their daily training routine.

Lightning, a huge, light chestnut stallion with a wide white blaze down his forehead, spotted O'Sullivan and Coffin as soon as they rounded the corner. He shook his head, whinnied, and then cantered along the rail to meet them. Phoebe, a large and extremely powerful grey mule of indeterminate age and lineage, followed the horse at a more leisurely gait; together they put their heads over the rail, received their carrots, and the usual obligatory petting, with much enthusiasm.

It was quite unusual for infantrymen to own horses, or mules for that matter, but certain allowances had been made for O'Sullivan and Coffin. Coffin had acquired Lightning for O'Sullivan, who was then the sergeant major; exactly how, from where, and from whom Coffin got the stallion, O'Sullivan didn't know nor did he want to know.

The mule, O'Sullivan had found for Coffin, and he wasn't saying from where, or how, either. Since then, the two animals had carried their masters more than two hundred miles across Northern Alabama; fought a half-dozen running battles, and carried them to freedom when Streight had finally been stopped by Nathan

Bedford Forrest outside of Rome, Georgia. All that had happened more than two years ago but the two men had been allowed to keep them for personal use.

The men saddled their animals, mounted, and rode back to O'Sullivan's tent. There, they checked their weapons: Coffin owned an 1860 .44 caliber Colt Army revolver and a seven-shot Spencer repeating rifle. O'Sullivan had two similar Colt revolvers—the theory being that one size ammunition would fit all three weapons. O'Sullivan also owned a ten-gauge Richards shotgun, courtesy of Coffin. The huge shotgun was usually loaded with buck and ball ammunition. Both men also carried Bowie knives, though Coffin's was much smaller than O'Sullivan's. They packed the weapons into the saddlebags, with the exception of the two long guns; these they would carry with them.

"How much cash do we have on hand, Boone?"

Without a moment's hesitation, Coffin answered, "We have nine hundred and eighty three dollars and seventy seven cents in cash. You have three thousand four hundred and ninety dollars in the bank in Nashville. I have ... well, I have a little more than that," he said with a sheepish grin.

O'Sullivan nodded thoughtfully, and then looked sharply at Coffin, when he realized what he had said.

"You have more than three thousand dollars in the bank?" he asked, incredulously. "How in the name of the Holy Mother did you manage that?"

"Well, now, Cap, that's a long story. But, to make it short, I never owned a buck I didn't double, and then some."

O'Sullivan smiled, nodded, and then said, "Right you are, me old son; right you are. An' well done. Well, now, the nine hundred should be enough, for now, at least. If we need more, I can get it from the paymaster at Fort Scott. I'm owed some back pay an' he'll do a bank draft, I'm sure."

"What about our clothes, Cap? We'll need civilian clothes, right?"

"No! We stay in uniform, at least until we know what we're about. He turned and grabbed the saddlebags, "Let's go, Boone."

"Yes, sir."

"Oh, and Boone, let's drop the sir and Captain stuff, at least while we're on our own. Call me Ronan."

"Yes, sir... er, Ronan. Ronan?" he said, his eyes wide, "I thought your name was Ignatius."

"It is. Ronan's me middle name, an' it's what Bonnie calls me, an' it's easier to say than Ignatius, and no one," he said, grimly, "I mean no one, not even you, Boone, calls me Iggy. Got it?

"Yessir, Cap... Ronan. Um, that's gonna take a lot o' gettin' used to. Cap is one thing, but first names ... well, I'll do me best."

"That you will, me old son. That you will."

They arrived at the railway yards in Nashville at a little after one o'clock in the afternoon and were pleased to find that a train to St. Louis was scheduled to leave at four o'clock. O'Sullivan bought tickets to Kansas City, with a change in St. Louis, and they set about loading the animals into a boxcar at the rear of the train.

Having made sure that the two animals were secure and happy, along with their saddles and the rest of the baggage, the two men settled themselves into the first carriage next to the one that housed the horses; Coffin did not intend to let them out of his sight until they arrived in Kansas City.

Chapter 3

April 9th, 1865 - Fort Scott, Kansas

The train carrying O'Sullivan and Coffin arrived in Kansas City during the mid-afternoon of April 6. The journey from Nashville, though it had taken only three days to travel the five hundred miles, had been long and tiresome, with many stops along the way. Still, the train ride had cut more than fifteen days off what would have been an interminably long ride, and by the time they arrived at their final destination, they were both well rested and ready for whatever might lie ahead, although, for most of the way, O'Sullivan had said very little. His mind was elsewhere; he was worried about his sister, and even more worried about her baby.

While the animals were being unloaded from the boxcar, Coffin took care of the baggage and checked the weapons Then together, they saddled up, and loaded the paniers onto the mule. The mule seemed not in the least uncomfortable under the extra weight.

They rode out of Kansas City at a little after four o'clock in the afternoon. With more than two hours of daylight left, O'Sullivan wanted to make a good start on the ninety-mile ride from Kansas City to Fort Scott before they camped for the night.

It was close to noon on Sunday April 9—three days after they departed Kansas City—when they rode through the gates of Fort Scott and into the compound.

Fort Scott was constructed in two sections: a stockade and a couple of dozen, or so, stone building: offices, barracks, a sutler's store, blacksmith's shop, officer's quarters, and so on; all surrounding a vast parade ground, upon which, two very loud sergeants were putting two companies of infantry through their paces.

Beyond and outside the perimeter to the east were more barracks, several dozen civilian homes, and a large hospital facility that served not only the military contingent at the fort, but also the surrounding populace of two states—Kansas and Missouri. The hospital was manned by military personnel: doctors and nurses.

They were met at the gates by a lieutenant who first saluted O'Sullivan, then demanded to see their identification, and to know the purpose of their visit. Satisfied that all was in order, he directed them around the parade ground to the offices on the east side of the complex with instructions to report to Colonel Hiram Richard, the officer commanding Fort Scott. Coffin was asked to wait in the outer office while an orderly escorted O'Sullivan in to see the colonel.

"Good afternoon, Captain," Richard said, standing up behind his desk and returning O'Sullivan's salute. "I've been expecting you. You had a good journey, I trust. Take a seat, man. Cigar?"

O'Sullivan sat down on a leather chair in front of Richard's desk.

"No thank you, Colonel," O'Sullivan said, shaking his head at the offer of the cigar. "The journey, sir, was long and boring... My sister, sir?"

"Doing well, Captain, doing well, and so is the baby. Though he arrived a mite early; five weeks early, in fact; he's very small, bless him, but strong and healthy; he'll make it.

"Mighty lucky, though, she was. Shot in the left breast. Small caliber weapon; .36 Navy, I shouldn't wonder, and no doubt a faulty charge. Ball didn't penetrate more than a couple of inches. Yes, she's one lucky young woman. Her state of mind, though... well, that's not so good; but what can we expect? Raped, at least six times, shot, left for dead. And, she's lost her husband. He was shot in the head, and scalped, too, though she doesn't know about that yet. And, she never should know it, I think. Keep it to yourself, Captain. Keep it to yourself."

"I need to see her, Colonel. Now, if you please."

"Of course. I'll have Corporal Smith take you to her."

At that moment, Corporal Smith burst in through the door without knocking. He was waving a sheet of paper and shouting joyously, "It's over, Colonel. Telegraph from Kansas City. Lee's done surrendered to Grant; the war's over! Yipee!"

Both officers rose from their seats.

"Here, let me see that," Richard reached over his desk and took the paper from Smith.

"It's true, just an hour ago, at Appomattox." Richard dropped back into his seat and stared at the paper, his hand shaking. He put the paper down on the desk, leaned back in his chair, and stared up at the ceiling.

"Johnston is still fighting Sherman, so's Stand Watie still fighting to the west, and Sterling Price, but none of that can last; and there are some isolated Confederate units operating in Arkansas... and Quantrill's band of ruffians, well, we'll talk more about them later. But it's done, Captain, it's all but done.

"Well, that will all keep. Smith, take Captain O'Sullivan to see his sister. And, Captain, please take your time, but we do need to talk, and soon. If you would, when you're done, please return here. Now, go visit your sister, and give her my regards."

They found her sitting up in bed, three beds down on the right, dozing.

"I'll wait here," Coffin said, taking a seat just outside of the large women's ward. "Maybe... I can say hello... later?"

"Yes, give me a little time alone with her, and then I'll come an' get you."

O'Sullivan walked quietly into the ward. He rounded the end of her bed, sat down, reached over, and took her hand.

35

"Hey, Bonnie," he whispered.

She woke with a start. Frightened, she snatched her hand away before she recognized him.

"Oh, Iggy, you came," she said when she realized who it was.

He took her hand again, smiling, "Now, Bonnie, you know that no one calls me that, not even you."

"I've always called you Iggy, and I know you hate it. But, to me, for as long as I can remember—since long before we got on the boat back in Belfast—I've called you that; you'll always be my Iggy. Oh my, look at you, a captain an' all. Daddy would have been so proud... I'm so proud of you ..."

He looked down at the floor, then again at her face, "How's the wound, Bonnie? Is it healing?"

"Eh," she said, with a small shrug of her shoulders. "It's just about healed, look." She pulled the neck of her gown aside to reveal a nasty-looking, bright red scar just above her left breast. "See? It's nothing."

She covered the scar, was silent for a moment, then looked up at him, and whispered, "They... killed Gabe. They killed him; shot him in the head, right in front of me... And they *raped me*, over an' over."

She burst into tears.

O'Sullivan rose from his seat, stepped close to the bed, put his arms around her, gently, and held her. "Oh my love," he whispered. "I am so, so sorry."

36

She buried her head against his chest and stayed there for a moment. Finally, she pulled away and looked up into his eyes. "There's a baby, Iggy. I called him Michael; it's what Gabe wanted to call him, if it were to be a boy, after his father. Oh God, I miss him so."

She pushed him gently away, wiped the tears from her face with a corner of the bed sheet, and then waved to attract the attention of a nurse at the far end of the room.

O'Sullivan sat back down in the chair and stared at her. She looked so small, so frail, so... vulnerable. Then his eyes narrowed, he gritted his teeth, clenched his fists at his sides, and the anger welled up inside him; like bile in the back of his throat. His eyes watered as he tried to imagine what his baby sister must have endured, but he couldn't. *Oh, but they'll pay for it, so they will.*

"Here's you nephew, Iggy."

He came out of his reverie, turned and looked round and saw the nurse walking down the center of the room carrying a small bundle—a very small bundle. The nurse approached the bed and placed the infant in Bonnie's arms. She held him close, put her cheek next to his, kissed him with the side of her mouth, and again, began to cry.

O'Sullivan didn't know what to do.

"Come see him," she whispered.

He rose to his feet; stepped closer, leaned over the bed, and looked down at the tiny face. He smiled as he saw big blue eyes looking up at him.

"He looks like you."

"No, Iggy. He looks like you: the same nose, same blue eyes." She sniffed, and wiped her nose in the crook of her elbow, then the tears, on the sleeve of her gown.

"He's... beautiful, Darlin'. He'll be a fine one, so he will."

She cuddled the baby close to her chest, and, for a moment, neither one of them spoke. Finally, Bonnie broke the silence: "How's Boone? Is he well? Is he here? I know you two are inseparable."

"Yes, he's here; just outside. You want to say hello?"

"I do. Ask him to come on in."

O'Sullivan did as he was asked, and Coffin, hat in both hands in front of him, walked sheepishly into the room, and sat down on the other side of the bed.

"Hello, Bonnie. How are you feelin'?" He looked at the baby. "Can I?" He dropped his hat on the floor beside him and held out his hands.

She looked at Coffin through her tears. Without any hesitation, she smiled at him, and held the baby out for him to hold. He took him gently in the crook of his left arm, held him with the other, and sat down again as he gazed in wonder at the small face.

O'Sullivan said nothing. He simply looked at Bonnie, then at Coffin, and smiled, a hard, tight-lipped smile.

For several moments, they sat in silence. Coffin finally handed back the baby and said, quietly, "We're gonna get 'em, Bonnie. Ronan ain't said as much, not yet, but I knows him better'n he knows himself, an' we'll get 'em."

She looked sharply back and forth, from one to the other, and said, "NO! YOU WILL NOT!"

She was again in tears. "I just lost my husband. I will not lose you too. There were too many of them. They were soldiers. There's only two of you. I won't have it, you hear; I won't have it."

"Stop it, Bonnie," O'Sullivan said, giving Coffin a warning look. "You just take it easy. You gotta get well. You got responsibilities now." He looked at the infant in her arms and said, "That little bugger is gonna need his mother to be strong."

"He's also going to need his Uncle Iggy, and... his Uncle Boone." She looked at Coffin and smiled as she said it. He smiled back at her, then looked down at his feet, spotted his cap on the floor, reached down and picked it up, and began nervously twisting it around his fingers. When he looked again at her, she could see his eyes were watering, and she smiled reassuringly at him.

"I gotta use the john," he said gruffly. "I'll see you later, Bonnie." Then he rose to his feet and walked quickly out of the room.

"Bonnie," O'Sullivan said. "I need to go talk to the Colonel. I'll stop by and see you later. In the meantime, you go back to sleep, get some rest."

He stood, leaned over the bed, and kissed her on the forehead. Then he kissed the top of Michael Powell's head, turned and walked after Coffin, wiping his eyes as he went.

"Colonel Richard. Captain O'Sullivan is here."

"Show him in, Corporal."

O'Sullivan and Coffin stepped into the office. Richard looked at Coffin, then at O'Sullivan, questioningly, and waited.

"If you don't mind, Colonel," O'Sullivan explained, "I'd like Sergeant Coffin to sit in on this meeting; he needs to know what I know."

"Of course, Captain. Sit down. SMITH!" the corporal stuck his head around the door. "Bring another chair for the sergeant, if you would."

"Now, what can I do for you, Captain?"

"I need to know what happed, sir. Who shot my sister an' killed her husband?"

"Yes, I'm sure you do. Well, it's easy enough to tell. A band of Confederate criminals, some of Quantrill's old

40

gang, led by a Lieutenant, Jesse Quintana, attacked Elbow. They... well, they did what they did to your sister, killed three of the townsfolk, including Mr. Powell and the preacher. They robbed every building in town, locked more'n fifty of the folk in the church, including almost a dozen children, and then set it afire. Fortunately, the Reverend Jones, the preacher, managed to sound the alarm before they killed him, and one of the townsfolk was able to ride to the fort for help. My men arrived just in time to save 'em, with exception of Jones and your sister's husband, of course, and another man they found in the store, a customer, I imagine.

"Your sister was in bad shape when they brought her in; thought early on that we might lose her, but no. She's a tough one; she pulled through, and so did the baby, thank the Lord.

"The raiders got away, though. I have troops out searching for them, but I'm afraid they are long gone."

"This... Quintana, and his band, what do we know about them?"

"They are bad bunch. Quintana... well, he's the worst of the worst. They were all members of Quantrill's gang. They call themselves partisan rangers, but they are scum: bushwhackers, thieves, criminals. I'm sure you've heard what happened at Lawrence, yes?"

O'Sullivan nodded his head. *Who the hell hasn't?*

"Of course you have," Richard continued. "Well, they were all there. This bunch, Quintana's, was part of

Bloody Bill Anderson's command. Anderson was a sadistic and merciless killer, one of the worst. When Anderson was killed a while back in Centralia, his command went to a Captain Arch Clement, another bad son-of-a-bitch. Quintana was Clement's second in command and, bad as Clement is, and he's still out there, too, somewhere, Quintana is ten times worse. He's an animal. He's fearless, brutal, kills without thought or reason and... he takes scalps, as well you know, and his men are almost as bad.

"Anyway, he had a falling out with Clement, and they went their separate ways. Now we have both factions to contend with, but separately, of course. Clement is somewhere in northern Missouri; Quintana? God only knows where he is. But, we'll get 'em; that I promise."

"How many are they, Colonel?"

"Quintana? Not sure. Twenty, maybe twenty-five."

O'Sullivan stood. "Well, I thank you, Colonel, so I do, but we'll be on our way. If it's all right with you, we'll stay the night here in the fort, say goodbye to Bonnie in the morning, and be away after breakfast."

"Sit down, Captain."

O'Sullivan sat, and looked stoically at Richard.

"I know what you're thinking, Captain," Richard said, quietly, shaking his head. "What are your plans? You can't be thinking of going after Quintana, I hope. He's more'n you can handle, just the two of you."

"Well, now, Colonel. The man has to pay for what he's done, so he does."

"Yes, but...."

"No buts, with respect, sir. He violated my sister, would have killed her, but for the hand o' God, an' he killed a good man, Gabe Powell, not to mention the preacher. He has to pay, and I intend to make him do just that."

Richard looked first at O'Sullivan, and then at Coffin, whose mouth was tightly clamped shut. He nodded his head, "Well, Captain. I can't stop you. Your leave of absence is open-ended, and it's signed by General Thomas, so time is not a problem."

He thought for a moment, and then continued, "I want Quintana as badly as you do. I will telegraph a request to Colonel Streight and General Thomas that you be temporarily attached to the 14th Kansas Cavalry. If your detachment is approved, which I'm sure it will be, I'll let you have a short company of cavalry, and a lieutenant with, say, fourteen men and a scout; I cannot spare more than that.

"I'll also draft specific orders; your mission will be to track down and arrest, or kill, this band of renegades. In the meantime, while we're waiting for a reply, I suggest you get some rest, spend some time with your sister.... SMITH!"

Again, the corporal stuck his head around the door.

"Yes, sir?"

"Go and find Colonel Johnson and Lieutenant Warwick of the 14th and have them report to me here as soon as possible. Whoa, just a moment before you go rushing off."

Richard grabbed a pen and paper and scribbled rapidly for a few moments.

"Make five copies," he said, handing the paper to Smith, "and have them on my desk, quick as you can. Then send this to Nashville," he handed Smith a second sheet of paper. "Now go!

"You, Captain, Sergeant, will go and get something to eat and then report back to me at, say..." he looked at the clock on the wall, "four o'clock. Johnson and Warwick should be here by then. Off you go."

O'Sullivan and Coffin arrived back at Richard's office right on time. The small room felt a little crowded; Lieutenant Colonel Johnson and Lieutenant Warwick were already seated, but all three men stood when they walking in and introductions were made.

"Sit down, gentlemen," Richard said, seating himself. He began shuffling through the papers on his desk, found the one he was looking for, and then continued, "Captain, I have received a telegraph from General Thomas in response to my request. You are both now temporarily attached to the 14th Kansas Cavalry and as such are, technically, at least, under the command of Lieutenant Colonel Johnson for as long as the current

44

assignment shall last. You will, however, report directly to me.

"I also received word from General Thomas that you, Sergeant Coffin, have received a promotion, effective April 1st. Congratulations, Sergeant Major."

O'Sullivan slapped Coffin on the shoulder, and congratulations were offered all round; Coffin opened his mouth to speak, hesitated, grinned sheepishly, changed his mind, and then said nothing.

"Now, let's get to the matter in hand," Richard said, looking at all four men in turn. "You will have no official standing in the 14th, per se, Captain. I have, however, already discussed this situation with Colonel Johnson and he has agreed to the following: you will have assigned to you a section of Company C, twelve troopers. Unfortunately, under the present circumstances, we can't spare more than that. Lieutenant Warwick, here, will also be assigned to your command, along with Sergeant Jedidiah Holmes, and an Osage scout, skilled in the art of tracking, something you'll need, of that I have no doubt. You will also be provided with three pack animals and supplies enough to last for two weeks, should you need more, you will be at liberty to purchase whatever you need in the field."

Richard paused, looked each of them in the eye, then continued, "Any questions so far?"

Lieutenant Warwick, looking far from happy, said, "How long is this... this assignment supposed to last, Colonel?"

O'Sullivan turned and looked at him, but said nothing; Warwick did not meet his gaze.

"For as long as it takes, Lieutenant," Richard replied. "It's been ten days since Quintana hit Elbow. Ten days... he could be anywhere."

"Sir," Warwick said, "In ten days, they could have travelled more than three hundred miles. They are probably gone from the state by now. I do not see how we can even find 'em, much less catch 'em."

There was no mistaking the skepticism in his voice, but O'Sullivan thought he heard a hint of something else as well...

Richard looked hard at Warwick. "If I were you, Lieutenant, I would let Captain O'Sullivan worry about that."

Warwick opened his mouth to speak again, but thought better of it and remained silent.

O'Sullivan watched him out of the corner of his eye; the man's face was red. Was he angry? Embarrassed? O'Sullivan could not decide which.

"Your orders, Captain," Richard said, handing him three sheets of paper folded together, "are to pursue the outlaw Jesse Quintana and his gang, and either capture or kill them. Should it be the latter, there will be no repercussions; if it be the former, you will bring them in, or whatever survivors of the gang there may be, for trial and punishment.

"Now, Captain," he said to O'Sullivan, but he looked at Lieutenant Warwick, "it is highly probably that yours will be an extended expedition, perhaps several months; no matter; these bastards must be caught and neutralized, and quickly. You leave at first light on Tuesday morning; that gives you thirty-six hours to prepare. Whenever possible, you will report your progress to me via telegraph. Questions?"

"Colonel," O'Sullivan said. "What of Quintana's whereabouts? Do you have any idea at all where he might have gone?"

"All we know is that he left Elbow heading west toward Eureka, but somewhere along the way he seems to have disappeared. You will have to track him down, Captain; track him down. He has ten day's start. Anything else?"

There were no more questions, or comments; everyone in the room, with the exception of Lieutenant Warwick, was a veteran soldier with experience enough to know and understand what was needed.

"Well then. I suggest you go and prepare. You, Captain, go get to know your men; say your goodbyes to your sister, and please... give her my best wishes and tell her I'll drop by and see her soon. Oh, and by the way, Captain, I will personally see to her disposition and welfare when she is released by her doctor, so you need have no concerns about that."

The four men rose to leave. As they did so, Richard stopped them, "If you don't mind, Lieutenant Warwick, I'd like a word."

He waited until O'Sullivan, Coffin, and Colonel Johnson had left, and the door was closed, and then said, "Sit down, Lieutenant, we need to talk."

Warwick sat; he looked decidedly uncomfortable.

"What the hell was that all about?" Richard asked, angrily.

"What do you mean, sir?"

"You know exactly what I mean. I could tell by your tone that you do not like Captain O'Sullivan. You want to explain?"

"Colonel...." He hesitated, then said, abruptly. "No sir! I do not."

"Well, let me give you a little advice, Sonny. O'Sullivan might be a little rough around the edges... Oh, I see. Is that what this is about, that he's an Irishman?"

Warwick sat stiffly upright in his chair, but said nothing.

"Hah. You think the man is not officer material."

Again, Warwick declined to answer.

"Well now, Mr. West Point. I think you are going to have a real problem, and I also think it might be best if you tried to hide your feelings. Both General Thomas and Colonel Streight think very highly of Captain O'Sullivan, which should tell you something."

"With respect, Colonel, the man is...."

"Enough, Lieutenant," Richard interrupted him angrily. "Who, and what, the hell do you think you are? Captain O'Sullivan is a highly experienced soldier. He earned his rank under fire through a dozen battles.

"The man fought in every major battle from Shiloh to Franklin, which is where he received his commission, and that, only after almost every other eligible officer in his brigade had either been killed or too severely wounded to remain on the duty roster; the man is a hero. What right have you, a shave tail lieutenant, barely wet behind the ears, to be questioning whether or not he deserves it?

"You will, at all times, and under all circumstances, carry out the captain's orders without question, and to the best of your ability. Now get out of here. You make me sick."

"So," Bonnie said, looking up at him. "You're going after them."

O'Sullivan nodded. "Yes, I have to. They have to be stopped; but you'll be fine, so you will. The medical folks here are the best there is, an' Colonel Richard has promised to keep an eye you."

"Ronan, I know that. It's not me I'm worried about, it's you."

49

"There's no need. I have a company of cavalry and Boone, and a very fierce young lieutenant," he said, grimly, "so all will be well. But you, what will you do when you get out o' here?"

"I'll go back to the store, of course, and reopen it. Gabe and I put everything we had into it, we... that is I, own it, free and clear, and I'll need somewhere to live, somewhere for Michael, something to keep me busy, take my mind off of...."

O'Sullivan nodded. "Sure you will, an' it's a good plan. Now look, if there's anythin' you need, anythin' at all. You go straight to Colonel Richard an' request it. I'll make sure he knows that I'll pick up the tab when I return." *If I return.*

"I'll be back as soon as I can. In the meantime, don't you worry about a thing. All will be well."

He bent over her, kissed her on the forehead, then turned abruptly and walked quickly from the ward. Boone Coffin was waiting outside.

"Ronan," he said, as O'Sullivan clapped him on the shoulder. "I've been thinkin'. I think, perhaps, you an' me; we should talk about the lieutenant."

"What about him?"

"Be best, perhaps, if we leave him behind. He could be more trouble than he's worth."

"Nah, cain't leave him. He's young, Boone—no experience; all West Point an' spit an' polish, so I hear, and full of piss and vinegar, too. 'Sides, it wouldn't be right to ruin the lad's career before it's begun. You an' me, we'll soon whip him into shape. He'll be fine."

Coffin was not convinced. "Ronan, he had the cajones to speak up, not only in front of Johnson, but Colonel Richard too."

"That, me old son, is true, very true, but it could also be a good thing. If he ain't afraid of his officers, then he might just do well under fire. An' I have a terrible strong feelin' that it's them kind of cajones we are gonna be needin' when we catch up with Quintana."

Chapter 4

April 12, 1865 - Great Bend, Kansas

Quintana's lead was not as great as O'Sullivan thought. When he, O'Sullivan, left Fort Scott on the morning of April 11, Quintana, was some forty miles east of Great Bend on the Santa Fe Trail; his plan was to head south and cross the border into Mexico. The gap between them was less than two hundred and forty miles, give or take, seven, perhaps eight day's ride, depending upon the weather, and how hard they pushed the horses.

When Quintana and his crew had left Elbow on the afternoon of March 30, they had headed west toward Eureka, but then turned north, instead, and headed toward Emporia. For thirty miles, they rode northward, and then, staying well out of sight, the raiders had turned again, by-passed Emporia to the south, and then turned west onto the Santa Fe Trail.

Quintana was indeed a master of the "game of war." Not only did he send two scouts on ahead, he also sent two more to the rear to watch for pursuit and, as none was observed, he had slowed his pace to little more than a walk.

Their route westward roughly followed the Santa Fe Trail, but they avoided all of the population centers, until, twelve days later, on April 12, they were within fifteen miles of Fort Zarah, the home of the Federal 2nd

Regiment of Colorado Cavalry, and the town of Great Bend.

It was there, early in the afternoon, that one of Quintana's forward scouts spotted a small group of Federal Cavalry heading west toward the fort.

"Sir, enemy cavalry," the scout shouted as he hauled his horse to a skidding stop in front of Quintana, "'bout a half mile ahead, on the trail headin' west."

"How many of 'em, son?"

"Six, sir, on'y six; a sergeant and five troopers, an' they's a tootlin' 'long just as nicely as y'may please."

"Well, let's go get 'em, boys," shouted Sergeant Brown.

"Brown! Hey, now hold on there, Sergeant," Quintana shouted as Brown put spurs to horse, "not so damned fast. We'll get there soon enough. Take ten men an' circle through the grass to the south an' come up in front of 'em. Me an' the rest o' the boys will close up on their rear. When we heah's ya shootin', we'll come a runnin' an' box 'em in. Now go!"

Quintana stood up in the stirrups and watched as they rode away into the long grass.

"Now, boys, spread out an' form line abreast. We'll close up some on them blue bellies. Y'all stay back, behind me, 'bout a hundred yards. Keep your eyes on me. When I fire in the air, y'all come a runnin', y'heah?"

He spurred his horse and moved forward at an easy canter, opening a gap between him and the rest of his men.

No more than fifteen minutes later, he heard the sounds of gunfire away down the trail to the west. He raised his pistol in the air, fired a single shot, and then urged his horse to the gallop, the rest of his men in a long line on either side of the trail, followed behind him, weapons drawn, flailing their horses with their reins.

They were on them in less than a minute. Sandwiched between Quintana's two forces, the six Federal troopers had no chance. The sergeant had gone down at the first shot from Brown's carbine. A second trooper fell almost at the same time. The other four men, now completely surrounded, raised their hands in surrender.

"Howdy, boys," Quintana smiled as he said it, but there was no "glad to meet you" look in his eyes, just cold, dark hatred.

"Sir," one of the troopers said, with his hands in the air, "why are you doing this? The war's over. Don't you know that? We ain't enemies no more."

"Is that so? Is that so? Do tell. An' when did all this happen, young sir?"

"General Lee surrendered three days ago."

"You lyin' sack o' shit," Quintana shouted. "Ain't no way Lee would ever surrender!" He pointed the Colt at the man and shot him in the groin.

The trooper toppled sideways off his horse and lay on his back, holding his gut, and gasping. Slowly and deliberately, Quintana shot him twice more, once again in the gut, then with great care as the man stared up at him, in his right eye, killing him instantly.

Then, he turned in the saddle and looked at each of the three remaining troopers in turn, and growled, "Any of you boys got anythin' to say that might be worth listnin' to? No? Well then, there's no point in delayin' things. Get yourself outa them clothes. Do it now!"

With a smile, Quintana watched as the three men disrobed, dropping their uniforms on the ground beside them.

"Thank you, boys," he said, as he pulled back the hammer of his pistol. One after the other he murdered the three troopers where they stood.

"Now then," he said, to no one in particular. "Let's see what we got."

They stripped the rest of bodies, took their personal belongings; weapons, money, clothes, leaving them lying naked at the side of the trail.

"Hold on y'all," "Quintana said, as he walked to his horse. "We need to do a little coverin' of our tracks heah; don't want them boys at Fort Zarah thinkin' it was us that did this, now do we? Lay them out a little farther apart; make 'em look a little more natural like."

He untied the cords that held his bedroll together, rummaged around inside it, and then pulled out two arrows.

He walked back to the dead troopers, stood above the one he had shot in the eye, and pushed the steel tip of one of the arrows deep into the hole where his eye had been. The other arrow he pushed deep into the throat of a second trooper; took a step back, looked around, and admired his handiwork. Next, he took the Bowie knife from his belt; it took him only a couple of moments to scalp all six of the troopers. One after another, he grabbing the lock of hair at the front of the head, and then sliced away a strip of scalp from front to back, leaving the skull exposed and bloody. When he was done, he wiped the blood off the blade and returned the knife to his belt.

"That should do it," he said, wrapping the scalps in one of the dead trooper's shirts.

"Damned Cheyenne," he said, with a grin. "I hate them son's-o-bitches. Get mounted.

"Now then, y'all," he said, adjusting his buttocks on the two strips of hard leather that comprised the McClellan cavalry saddle. "The fort is 'bout fifteen miles thataway." He pointed along the Trail toward the west. "Cain't go that way; we need to stay clear o' the Federals: war over or not. There's an old side trail just down this here trail apiece that leads back to the Santa Fe south of the fort. So, let's get outa heah, an' quick."

The trail Quintana spoke of was less than a mile away from the scene of the massacre, and barely discernable. Two days later, by early morning on April 14, they were camped in a shallow defile, forty miles south of Fort Zarah and just five miles to the southwest of Fort Larned.

When the six troopers failed to return from their patrol, Colonel Edward McGarry, commanding the 2nd Cavalry at Fort Zarah, sent a search party to find them. The captain in charge of that search party finally found them late that afternoon and sent a rider back to McGarry with the news. The rider returned to the site of the massacre that same night at around ten o'clock with more men and a wagon to pick up the bodies. It was well past midnight when the sad little group rode into the fort; McGarry was waiting for them at the gates.

"Any idea what happened, Captain?" he asked.

"Indians, sir. Cheyenne, I'd say, by the look of the arrows. They was all stripped, robbed, and skelped, too."

"That doesn't seem possible," McGarry said, thoughtfully. "As far as I know, there's not been a Cheyenne dog soldier seen this side of the Arkansas River in more than six months."

"The arrows don't lie, Colonel. Take a look at the feathers, and the markings."

The captain pulled the two broken shafts from his belt and handed them to McGarry.

"Well, it certainly seems that way; the feathers are definitely Cheyenne."

He walked to the wagon and pulled back the canvas cover. He shuddered when he looked at the bodies of his six troopers.

"Captain, these men have been shot. The Cheyenne do not have guns, at least, not to my knowledge, they don't."

"Must have, Colonel," the captain replied. "But, they sure as hell are Cheyenne arrows."

'Get them looked after, Captain," McGarry said, covering the bodies. "Then send someone to my office. I'll have a message for command. He can take it into Great Bend, to the telegraph office. No doubt he'll have to wake the telegrapher, but it has to be done. Thank you, Captain."

McGarry, weary and dejected, returned the captain's salute, turned and walked slowly away, his head down, and his hands clasped behind his back.

Chapter 5

April 12, 1865 - West of Fort Scott, Kansas

It was barely daylight, and there was a sharp chill in the air when O'Sullivan and Coffin, now with the chevrons of his new rank sewn onto his shirtsleeves, stepped out onto the parade ground at Fort Scott where the men of his small command were already assembled and waiting.

Dawn was about to break and already the sky was streaked with of gold; the scudding white clouds overhead, were rimmed with red. It was going to be a beautiful day.

In line abreast, with Lieutenant Dilman Warwick, Sergeant Holmes, and a very tall Indian out in front, the twelve troopers of Company C stood patiently beside their horses. O'Sullivan's horse, Lightning, and Phoebe the mule were hitched to a rail outside the sutler's store; the three pack mules, already loaded, stood off to one side.

"At ease everyone, and good morning," O'Sullivan said, loud enough for all to hear, as he returned Warwick's salute.

"Is everything ready, Lieutenant?"

"It is, sir."

"Good, an' who might this be?" He asked, looking at the Indian scout; the man stood at least two inches taller than O'Sullivan.

"That's Big Man, Captain. He's Osage. Couldn't pronounce his real name, so that's what we call him."

Lieutenant Warwick was one of those good-looking young men that never seemed to have any trouble making their way through life. He came from a well-respected, upper class Philadelphia family and was accustomed to all of the privileges that went with it.

He'd graduated West Point in 1864, twentieth in his class of forty-two. He was twenty-three years old, tall, a little over six feet, with wavy brown hair, cut short just below his kepi and above his ears. His face was thin with wide-set hazel eyes. He was clean-shaven, except for a small mustache; his mouth was set in a semi-permanent, sardonic half-smile. His boots were polished to a high gloss, and he wore his shell jacket with the top two buttons undone.

He was well-spoken, fit and, to O'Sullivan's mind, looked disgustingly healthy... and he did not seem at all happy with his new assignment, nor did he appear to be impressed with his new commanding officer, and O'Sullivan was well aware of both.

"Big Man," O'Sullivan said, nodding to the Indian as he stepped around Warwick to stand in front of the men.

"By now," O'Sullivan said, "you men should have a good idea of what it is we're about. I cannot tell you exactly where we are goin', or how long we'll be gone. I will tell you, that we are gonna catch this Rebel son-of-a-bitch, no matter how long it takes.

"Y'all know who and what he is, an' what he's done. Elbow was just the latest in a long list of atrocities dating all the way back to the massacre at Lawrence. This is one evil son-of-a-bitch we're after: a brutal savage who takes no prisoners, kills for the love of it, an' don't think twice about it. He has a big start on us, almost two weeks, an' the only thing we know of his whereabouts is that when he left Elbow he was heading' toward Eureka. So, that's where we'll begin. Any questions?"

"Just one, Captain," Warwick said, with his ever-present half-smile. "It's for the Sergeant Major."

"Lieutenant?" Coffin asked, frowning.

"It's the mule, Sergeant. Would you like me to have it replaced with a horse?"

O'Sullivan grinned and looked sideways at Coffin, knowing what was coming.

Coffin's eyes narrowed menacingly as he asked, "And, why would I want you to do that, *sir*?"

"Well... it's a mule. They're slow, and... well, we *are* cavalry."

"Lieutenant," Coffin said, quietly. "Phoebe, that's the mule's name, has carried me through hell'n high water for the better part of two years. She carried me for more'n two hundred miles across north Alabama on Streight's Raid; you have heard o' that, right?"

Warwick nodded, still smiling.

"She was with me at Stones River, and at Chickamauga. She knows me and I knows her; never

61

once has she let me down. And, yeh, she's a might slow, but, by God, she'll still be on her feet and moving long after the last of those nags," he nodded in the direction of the rest of the troop, "has given up. No, sir, I would *not* like for you to replace her, but thank you for asking."

Warwick nodded, shrugged his shoulders, then turned to O'Sullivan, and said, "Your instructions, Captain."

"How about supplies?"

"We have rations for the men and horses for ten days and sufficient ammunition for, well... for whatever our immediate needs might be. We are ready to leave, Captain."

O'Sullivan nodded, took a deep breath, and then said, "Eureka is about ninety miles west of here. We should be there sometime late on Friday."

He looked around, turned and walked to the hitching rail, took Lightning's reins from the rail, swung himself easily up into the saddle and shouted, "Mount up! Move out!"

Five minutes later, with O'Sullivan at its head, the small column trotted through the gates and out of the fort.

The trail led west through Elbow, past the pile of ashes that had once been the church, past the graveyard with its three fresh graves, and past the general store—its doors closed, dark inside. O'Sullivan slowed his horse, stared at its facade, but he didn't stop; there was no point. Instead, he looked away, stared straight ahead, lightly touched his spurs to Lightning's flanks, urged the horse to a comfortable canter, and rode out of the small town and into the grasslands beyond; the troopers followed in close formation.

After an easy three-day ride, O'Sullivan's small troop rode into Eureka at just after three o'clock in the afternoon on Friday, April 14. It was just a tiny settlement; a dusty little collection of wooden buildings bordering the trail on either side, a tiny church with room inside for perhaps a dozen folk, and a tiny, one-room schoolhouse. The street, no more than a wide, dirt road, deeply rutted by the passage of an endless stream of wagons following the trail west to Santa Fe, was deserted, except for two men who sat together on barrelheads outside what might have passed for a store, although even that description was an exaggeration. They were sitting with their backs leaned against the storefront, hats pulled low over their eyes to ward off the afternoon sun, their arms folded across their chests.

O'Sullivan called a halt and ordered his men dismount and find water for the horses.

He swung his left leg over Lighting's ears and dropped easily onto the dirt road, led his horse to the front of the store, flipped the reins around the rail, and looked down at the two men who gazed up at him.

"Howdy," O'Sullivan said.

For a long moment, the three men exchanged stares, until, at last breaking the uncomfortable silence, the older of the two men said, "Howdy, Cap. What're yer a need'n?"

"I'm lookin' for a troop of Confederate cavalry, 'bout twenty of 'em. They would have passed this way ten days ago, maybe more. You boys seen anything like that these past two weeks?"

They looked at each other, their arms still folded, then, together, they shook their heads, "Nossir," the younger of the men said. "They didn't come this aways. Sounds like 'em fellers that hit Elbow a couple o' weeks back. Heared tell they kilt the preacher, an' the couple who ran the store, an' her 'spectin a baby an' all; burned the church to the ground, too, so they say. Bad business. We'd a seen a bunch like, fo' sure."

O'Sullivan nodded his head. He believed them, knowing that these two, and also the rest of the inhabitants of the small town, probably wouldn't have been left alive to tell about it, had the ruffians passed this way.

"Well, they surly did set out this way; must o' turned off the trail somewhere. Any ideas where they might be headed?"

"The on'y place they could a done that, fur as I knows, would be back east of here. They could a turned northeast, some six miles that way." He unfolded his arms and pointed back the way O'Sullivan and his men had come. "They coulda took the trail to Emporia, maybe, but they fur sure didn't get to heah."

"Where is everyone?" O'Sullivan asked. "You two all there is to this..." he looked around, then continued, "well, cain't hardly call it a town?"

"Nossir, most of the folks is home - siesta time - an' them that ain't sleepin' is out tendin' the cows; an' some... well, they just ain't heah."

O'Sullivan sighed, nodded, removed his hat and scratched the top of his head. He looked up and down the dusty road, "Is there any place we can get somethin' to eat?" he asked. "I could use a good home-cooked meal."

"Yessir. Ol' missus Makepeace might could cook fur ya, at a price, no doubt. She owns that big ol' house, up there on the left, toward the end o' town."

O'Sullivan unhooked Lightning and walked west along most of the length of the street—trail—whatever. The "big ol'" house turned out to be nothing more than a two story shack; two rooms, one above the other, age unknown, but "ol'" for sure.

He flipped the horse's reins around the rail and stepped onto the plank walkway in front of the house. The walkway, no more than a boardwalk front porch without a roof, began and ended at either end of the house.

O'Sullivan knocked on the front door, and waited. After a moment, he heard movement inside, then the clatter of bolts being drawn, three of them, and then the door opened to reveal a surprisingly well-dressed woman of about fifty years of age.

"Yeh, wadda ya want?" she said as she looked him up and down, and obviously was not impressed by what she saw.

"Mrs. Makepeace?"

She nodded. She was a large woman with a round face; large, full lips, piggy blue eyes, and a mass of fine gray hair, swept back and tied with a blue ribbon to reveal a pair of tiny ears adorned with long, dangling earrings. She was dressed in a voluminous, brown cotton dress of many layers, clean and pressed, that made her look even bigger than she actually was.

"That would be me," she said, her voice almost a squeak. "What kin I do fo' yuh?"

"The two gentlemen down the street suggested I come see you." He gestured toward the two men still sitting outside the store.

"Gentlemen, hah. Couple o' bums, more like. Never done a lick o' work they whole lives. So, what they tell ya?"

"They said that you cooked. Do you?"

"Depends, who for, for how many, and for how much."

"Just four of us, ma'am; me, my lieutenant and two sergeants. The rest of the boys will make camp outside o'

66

town an' do for themselves. I need a good home-cooked meal; ain't had one in more'n two weeks."

"Steak, taters an' greens wi' apple pie to foller, sound good?"

"Oh m'God. Yes ma'am."

"It'll cost ya a dollar-fifty a head. Be back here in an hour." She turned away and slammed the door in his face. Nevertheless, he grinned as he spun on his heel, jumped down off the porch, gathered Lightning's reins, and swung himself up into the saddle. Then, he rode slowly back down the street to where his men were still busy with the horses and pack animals.

They left at first light the next morning, heading east, back toward Elbow. By eight o'clock, they were already six miles out of Eureka, and had turned north onto the trail that led to Emporia.

The air was crisp and clean; the sky was a clear, pale blue, and it stretched endlessly to the horizon. A gentle breeze wafted over the boundless grasslands, turning them into a gently undulating ocean of dark green and russet browns. It was a beautiful morning.

O'Sullivan was in no hurry. He and the troop had breakfasted on fresh eggs, fatback bacon, and fried bread; all supplied by the obliging Mrs. Makepeace, for a price, of course, and washed down with several mugs of strong black coffee.

They were all well rested, the mood was upbeat, and the men were keen to be on their way, mostly because they were glad to be out of the fort and away from the drudgery of daily military life.

In column of twos, O'Sullivan leading, with Lieutenant Warwick to his left, Coffin to his right, followed by Sergeant Holmes and the scout, Big Man, they trotted easily along the well-defined trail.

"Have you had any thoughts," Warwick said, "about tactics when, and if, we find Quintana, Captain?"

O'Sullivan glanced sideways at his Lieutenant; he was staring directly ahead along the trail. O'Sullivan smiled, *and so it begins*, he thought.

"No Lieutenant. Cain't say that I have. Plenty of time to think about it, though. They could be a couple of hundred miles ahead of us, an' maybe more. And, what d'ya mean, if?"

"Well, sir. I'd say that with them having such a huge start on us, the chances of us even finding them are little to none."

"Oh, don't you worry none, Lieutenant. We'll find 'em all right. You need have no doubts 'bout that, none at all, not if it takes a year."

To his right, Boone Coffin smiled grimly, and nodded his head. To his left, Warwick, unseen by O'Sullivan, or so he thought, shook his head,

"Yes, sir!" The lieutenant said, less than enthusiastically.

"You sound doubtful, Lieutenant."

"Er... No, sir. Well, not so much. It's just that Quintana knows these parts, probably better than any of us, and he's skilled in guerilla tactics. He's been a bushwhacker since before the war began. If he catches us before we... Well, you get my drift, sir, I'm sure."

"That I do, Lieutenant, that I do," O'Sullivan turned in the saddle to look at him. "You got something' on your mind, Lieutenant? If so, spit it out. This ain't no time to be harboring a resentment."

"No, sir," Warwick lied, quickly, "absolutely not."

"That's good," O'Sullivan said, not believing a word of it, and lowering his voice so that only Warwick and Coffin could hear, "because I need to be able to rely on my second in command under any an' all circumstances, an' if I cain't, then you'd be better off heading back to the fort now, rather than later."

"You need have no concerns, Captain," Warwick replied, stiffly. "I will carry out my duties, as required."

"Not good enough, Lieutenant. As I said, I need to be able to rely on you, not just to do your duty, but to go above an' beyond, should there be a need, and there *will* be a need, of that you can be sure."

"You have my word, sir."

Coffin and O'Sullivan looked at one another. Coffin, unseen by Warwick, rolled his eyes. O'Sullivan merely nodded.

Chapter 6

April 16, 1865 - Santa Fe Trail South of Fort Dodge

By noon on the 16th, four days after the massacre at Fort Zarah, Quintana's raiders were approaching the Cimarron Route of the Santa Fe Trail, several miles to the south and west of what was soon to become Fort Dodge. They were taking their time, sure that they had covered their tracks, and that the Cheyenne would be blamed for the attack on the Federal patrol; they believed that a pursuit was unlikely.

When they left the bodies of the six Federal troopers beside the trail east of Fort Zarah, they had continued east for a little more than a mile. There, they had left the Santa Fe, and turned south onto a narrow, barely defined trail that led deep into the grasslands. The long, circuitous route meandered first to the south, and then swung toward the west, skirting the town of Great Bend and then Fort Larned, until, four days later, they rejoined the Santa Fe Trail some five miles to the southwest of Fort Dodge. As usual, Quintana had posted scouts a mile to the front and to the rear.

When the lead scouts reached the Trail, one of them turned north, as per his instructions, and headed toward Fort Dodge, for, in Quinatana's words, a 'look see.'

The afternoon was hot and sticky, quiet, with a light breeze blowing from west to east, barely stirring the tops of the grasses on either side of the Trail. The road was wide, the hard-packed dirt undulating, rutted, and dusty. It was bounded on both sides by dense grassland. In some places, the grass was so high that, even on horseback, it was impossible to see much beyond a few hundred yards in any direction. In other places it was sparse, the terrain rocky, more desert than grassland.

The scout had not gone far when, as he cantered around a sharp bend in the Trail, he ran slap into a Federal cavalry patrol, out from Fort Dodge five miles farther on.

Fortunately, he had his wits about him; the Federals did not. Surprised as he was, as soon as he spotted them, he hauled on the reins, dragged the horse around in a skittering turn, banged his spurs into the animal's flanks and, with a loud whinny, it leaped into the air, landed on all four hooves, and took off at full gallop, leaving the startled troopers staring after him.

But, they didn't stare for long. Within seconds, the entire troop, forty men, were also at full gallop, but the scout managed to hold his own, and soon the gap between them began to widen.

Quintana and the rest of his small force had already turned south onto the Trail and, upon hearing the approaching hoof beats, he called a halt, then rode back to the rear of the troop, just as the scout came tearing around the bend.

The scout, in a state of great agitation, hauled on the reins and the horse came violently to a stop, twisting sideways, his rider barely managing to stay in the saddle.

"Federal cavalry, sir," the man shouted, gesturing with his gloved hand in the direction from which he had just come. "A whole bunch of 'em, an' comin' fast."

"DISMOUNT! GET OFF THE DAMNED TRAIL!" Quintana shouted, but it was too late. Barely were the raiders out of the saddle when the Federals came storming around the bend.

When they saw Quintana's men scrambling to find some sort of defensive position, and making ready to fight, they also halted, but then quickly turned, fell back, and dismounted. Now on foot, they ran back toward the still disorganized Confederates.

Quintana's men, sixteen of them, were by now, most of them, down on one knee on either side of the trail. The rest of his men had retreated several hundred yards along the Trail to the south, and were handling the horses. As with most modern cavalry units, Federal or Confederate, Quintana's men always fought dismounted, as infantry. They were armed with Henry repeating rifles, all of them stolen from dead Union soldiers over a period of several years.

The Henry was the ideal cavalry weapon. It was a sixteen-shot (17 if a round was kept in the chamber), .44 caliber, repeating rifle, with a rate of fire restricted only by the speed with which its user could operate the lever.

Unfortunately for Quintana, not only were his men armed with repeating rifles, so were the approaching Federal troopers, although theirs were seven-shot Spencers, and they outnumbered him almost two-to-one.

The Federals also had another advantage; after three years fighting Indians, they were well used to their wily ways, and caution, for them, the Federal troopers, was the first order of battle on any and every level. Thus, instead of attacking head on down the road, Captain Pearce—the leader of the Federal troop—split his men into three sections. The first group of twelve men, he sent into the grassland to the right, the second he sent to the left, each with orders to circle around and try to come up on the enemy's rear; the third group, the bulk of his force, stayed with Pearce, on the trail, and waited.

"HO THERE." Pearce shouted.

There was no reply.

"HEY, JOHNNY. THE WAR'S OVER. NO NEED FOR A FIGHT. WE HAVE YOU OUTNUMBERED. THROW DOWN YOUR WEAPONS..."

He was interrupted by a burst of gunfire that swept over his head, the Minié balls wining like a swarm of angry hornets. Pearce did not return fire. Instead, he waited.

Quintana's men maintained a steady rate of fire, useless though it was; they couldn't see anything beyond the bend in the Trail. Then, some hundred yards away to the left, there was a crackle of gunfire from a dozen Federal rifles. Pearce's men had found Quintana.

Two of Quintana's men went down immediately; one was killed outright, the other with a Minié ball through his lower forearm, smashing both the ulna and the radius bones.

Quintana was taken by surprise. Even so, he was not a man to panic; he was a skilled battlefield commander, and a master of his favorite tactic, the retreat.

"GET OUTA HEAH, NOW!" he shouted, running, head down, his body low to the ground, waving his hat in the air to show his men the way.

They needed no more urging. They all upped and ran to the rear as fast as they could go, grabbed their horses, swung themselves into the saddle, and then tore off along the Trail at full gallop, but not before another of Quintana's men spun sideways out of the saddle, a ball through his neck, severing both his windpipe and carotid artery; he was dying, even as he hit the ground.

Two more of his men were also seriously wounded: one was hit in the calf of his right leg, the ball passing through from rear to front, shattering the fibula and tearing a huge exit wound; the other man, a corporal, took a ball in the lower right side of his back; it did not pass through.

For more than a mile, with Quintana and Brown in the lead, the fleeing Confederate raiders kept up the frantic pace until, without slowing, Quintana wrenched his horse to the right and, with his men streaming behind, galloped across the wasteland toward a low range of mountains some three miles, or so, to the west.

The Federals, slow to reach their horses, and now, more than a half-mile behind them, followed the guerillas along the Trail until they reached the point where they had left it, and there, Pearce reluctantly called a halt. In the distance, he could see the cloud of dust raised by the fast moving Confederates, but he decided not to follow. Quintana was heading deep into Indian country, and his orders forbade him to leave the Trail by more than a half-mile; Quintana was already that far away, and more.

Pearce regrouped his men, caught the two horses that had belonged to the two dead Confederate troopers, slung the two bodies across the saddles, and then headed northeast, back toward Fort Dodge.

Quintana and his men, now in the foothills of the mountains, had slowed their mounts to a fast trot. He called a halt, dismounted, took his field glasses from the leather pouch on his saddle, climbed a short way up the rocky slope, turned, and then scoured the terrain between them and the Santa Fe Trail, now almost four miles away: nothing. He nodded his head, satisfied that they were not being pursued, and then climbed down from his perch and rejoined his men.

"Goddamn," he growled, dropping to the ground, and laid flat on his back, his face to the sun. "That was close, too Goddamn close. Good work, Flint," he said to the scout that had given the warning. "Christ, that was close."

He lay there for several minutes; his men, now dismounted, also lay down on the ground or sat on rocks around him; some drinking water, some smoking cigars, all were exhausted.

A moment or two later, Quintana sat up, leaned back on his elbows, grinning, his head back as far as it would go.

"Weehooo," he shouted, into the air. "We done it again, boys. We done give 'em the slip. We'll find a place somewhere in these heah rocks an' make camp, rest up a while, an' then we'll head for Mexico. The war's over, leastways, so them blue bellies said, an' I has a hankerin' for one of them dusky little maidens, an' a few days o' peace an' quiet. It's bin a long four years, an' I'm mighty tired."

He lay back down, stared up at the clear blue sky, thinking.

"Sergeant Brown," he said, without taking his eyes away from the sky. "What is the condition of Jackson, Willis, and Burke? How are they doin'?" He was talking about the three wounded men.

"Jackson's not doin' so well, Lieutenant. He took a ball in the back, an' he's got blood in his mouth. Musta bin hit in the lung. He ain't gonna make it, so I b'leave. Willis is gonna lose his right arm; it's entirely shattered. He needs a hospital bad. Burke, he got shot in his right leg; ball went right on through, but it tore a damned huge hole on its way out, an' there's bits o' bone stickin' out; I dunno 'bout him either."

Quintana raised himself up onto his elbows once more, squinted up at his sergeant, shook his head and said, "Go finish 'em off, Brown," he spoke quietly. "They ain't gonna get to no hospital, not out heah. They ain't gonna make it, an' they'll just slow us down. Make it quick for 'em. One each in the ear. Give me a minute an' I'll take the rest o' the men outa heah."

Brown nodded, despondently, but he was not at all surprised at the order.

"You men grab the horses an' follow me," Quintana said, rising from the floor and mounting his horse. "We'll find a place to camp. Make your way over that way. Jackson, Willis, Burke; y'all stay heah. Sergeant Brown's gonna see what he can do to patch y'all up."

Quintana and the remaining sixteen troopers rode slowly along the rocky trail that led through the foothills and deeper into the mountains. They had not gone far when they heard three sharp cracks of a pistol. Not a word was said. Each and every one of them knew what had happened, and each and every one of them had expected no less.

High on top of the mountains to the northwest, unseen by Quintana and his men, a single puff of white smoke rose into the still, warm air. It was followed a moment later by another, and then another.

Chapter 7

April 19, West of Fort Dodge

Lieutenant Jesse Quintana was in a somewhat pensive mood as he led his small force through the foothills of the mountains some four miles to the west of the Santa Fe Trail, and thirty-five miles southwest of Fort Dodge.

About his dead companions, he gave not a thought, but he was worried. He well knew that after his encounter with the Federal cavalry three days ago, pursuit was more than likely. Thus he planned to stay well away from the known trails and stick to the foothills, but that brought with it new problems.

The going was slow; they were now averaging less than fifteen miles a day; and supplies were running low. Water was plentiful in the mountains; food was not. Hunting, however, at least for the present, was out of the question, for several reasons, the most important of which was that it would give away their position to any possible pursuers.

They did, however, have plenty of ammunition, having robbed the store in Elbow, and the six troopers at Fort Zarah. Each man was carrying no less than six hundred rounds, a burden all its own, but one they were not likely to give up, for it was unlikely they would find new supplies of the .44 caliber copper cartridges this side of El Paso, which was almost six hundred miles away.

Quintana was not, however, particularly worried about any bands of hostile Indians that might be in the area—the smoke signals on the mountaintops had not gone unnoticed for long. He simply did not respect or fear them, regarding them as little more than savages armed with inferior weapons and, for the most part, he was right; firearms among the tribes were, at least in these parts, uncommon.

Throughout the day, the small band of Confederate soldiers headed slowly southwest, paralleling the Santa Fe Trail, through the foothills of the mountains. By late afternoon, with the sun hanging low over the peaks and bluffs, they were almost fifty miles from Fort Dodge and Quintana was feeling relatively safe from pursuit, at least from the Federals.

"Whoa!" Quintana held up his hand, signaling for the column to stop. They were in a shallow defile paralleling the mountains, maybe a hundred feet above the grasslands to their left.

"Quiet! Look. Over there." He pointed with his right hand while reaching across the saddle with his left to grab his glasses.

There were between thirty and forty of them, Indians, travelling east in a column.

Quintana stared through his glasses, constantly adjusting the focus to try to combat the haze that hung over the waving ocean of grass.

There were nine warriors on ponies. The rest were women, fourteen, maybe fifteen of them—it was difficult to tell because of the distance—and children. They were all walking beside the travois; the children, some eight or nine young boys and girls of varying ages, were also on foot.

"Comanche, I think. Here, take a look." He handed the glasses to Sergeant Brown.

"Yessir, Comanches. I count maybe eight or nine bucks; the rest are women an' kids" he said, handing the glasses back to Quintana.

Quintana nodded his head and said, "They're headin' this way.

Dismount, *quietly!* Take cover. Them redskins got food, an' we need it."

"I dunno, Lieutenant," Brown said, shaking his head, worriedly. "If them's Comanche, you can bet there's a war party not far behind, or maybe in front. Takin' their womenfolk down may not be such a good idea."

Quintana looked hard at him.

"You goin' sour on me, Brown? Wettin' yo' britches over a bunch o' savages? So what if there's a war party. How many of 'em can there be? Fifty, Sixty, a hundred? An' them armed on'y with bows an' arrows an' sharp sticks. Why, with our Henry's we can pick 'em all off, them few down there, from heah before they knows what hit em, an' the same goes for any war party that might happen by. Goddamn it, Sergeant, we're vet'ran Confederate soldiers. They're just no account redskins. Pull yourself together, man."

Brown was not convinced, but he didn't argue. Instead he pulled his Henry rifle from its scabbard, checked the load, found himself a secure spot behind a large boulder, and sat down to wait.

The rest of Quintana's men also hunkered down behind the rocks, and waited. Their elevated position provided an uninterrupted view across the vast reaches of the grasslands; and all was quiet, even the birds seemed to have stopped singing. As far as the eye could see: nothing was moving, except for the small party of Comanche and the waving grass. Quintana, lying on top of a flat rock, his Henry rifle beside him, his glasses to his eyes, continued to watch the Comanche's progress.

The Confederate horses were back in the defile, out of sight, in the charge of the youngest member of the band, Johnny Ike, a tall, skinny, individual with a shock of dark red hair that stuck out at all angles from under a blue Federal kepi. The kepi, two sizes too big for him, was a souvenir from the raid at Fort Zarah; Ike, though he was just eighteen years old, and looked more boy than man, was already a seasoned killer.

The Comanche's progress was slow. Quintana was becoming restless, as were his men; Brown was not the only one who doubted the wisdom of what they were about to do.

Still more than a mile away from Quintana's positions, the Comanche were unaware that they were being watched.

Their leader, a minor chief, perhaps thirty years old, wore a headdress made from the skin of a buffalo head and neck, with its horns still attached; the flap of hide hung halfway down his back. His hair hung in two long, thick braids over his shoulders on either side of his chest, almost to his waist; a third braid, much finer than the other two, and his scalp lock was hidden beneath the headdress. He wore buffalo hide moccasins, buckskin leggings, decorated with strips of colored cloth, a thick leather belt that secured his breach cloth, and a vest made from tanned and shaved buffalo hide partially covered his otherwise bare chest. His wrists were decorated with bands of colored leather and polished circlets of metal that glinted in the sunlight. His skin was the color of weathered copper and his face was painted: yellow on the left side, red on the right. At his left side, he wore a buckskin scabbard that held a large, steel-bladed knife, double-edged, with a flat bone handle. Under his right armpit, he carried a war lance, across his back, a bow and a quiver of arrows; he was a formidable looking warrior.

The rest of the Comanche men were younger, late teens to early twenties; none wore headdresses; their hair was parted down the center and hung in plaited locks over their shoulders; their faces were painted a variety of colors, all were bare chested; all were armed with bows and lances.

The women were covered from head to toe in flowing shirts and skirts; on their feet, they wore moccasins; their hair was cut short, and parted in the middle. The boy children were naked but for a breach cloth; the girls were covered: cloth shirts and skirts.

It took the slow-moving group of Comanche another thirty minutes before Quintana was able to see exactly what he was up against, and another thirty before they came into range.

"Not a firearm among 'em," he muttered to himself, a satisfied grin on his face.

"Hold your fire, boys, 'til I give the word."

And, lying flat on his belly on top of the flat rock, the stock of the Henry rifle against his right cheek, the finger of his right hand caressing the trigger, his left eye closed as he sighted the weapon on the Comanche chief, he waited, and he waited, then...

BAM! The rifle slammed back into his shoulder. The Comanche, now less than two hundred yards away, pitched backwards out of the saddle. The rest of the party were taken completely by surprise.

"NOW!" Quintana yelled, jacking another cartridge into the chamber.

As one, the other seventeen rifles exploded, and the eight braves went down, almost together, so did four of the women. The ponies scattered, running off in all directions. Three of the horses reared in panic, then bolted off across the grasslands, dragging their travois behind them. The rest of the party stood still, bewildered, frightened.

"Well now," Quintana said, rising to his feet. "That was easy. Let's go see what we have."

Quintana and his men dropped down from the ridge and into the defile, running for the gap in the rocks to the narrow trail down onto the plain below.

On the plain, a young Comanche boy, perhaps thirteen years old, was down on one knee, both of his hands on the floor in front of him. He looked wildly around, saw the gun smoke rising from the ridge above the defile, and, seeing nothing moving, made up his mind, jumped to his feet and ran.

For nearly a hundred yards, the boy ran as fast as he could go to where one of the ponies was standing, head down, ears flat. It took him less than twenty seconds to reach the animal. When he did, without slowing, and with a mighty leap, he was up onto the pony's back and streaking away at full gallop, and he only just made it.

CRACK. Wheeee. The ball flew past his head, followed quickly by another, and another. But the boy, now flat on his belly on the pony's back, his face clamped to the left side of its neck, was too fast of a moving target, and the gap between him and Quintana's men was widening with every stride. A minute later, he was almost out of sight, well out of range of the Confederate rifles.

"GODDAM!" Quintana shouted. He was all but jumping up and down with rage.

"Leave the goddam ponies. See what's on those, those ... carts, whatever they are. FOOD, we need food."

He stood, legs akimbo, rifle in hand by his side, staring at the diminishing cloud of dust moving quickly to the south. *Damn, damn, damn, damn.*

For a long moment, he stood, silently, then he turned his attention to his men. They had gathered the women and children into a group and were now rifling through the goods and chattels on the travois. They flung anything they considered to be of no use to one side and stacked the hide-bound packages of dried meat, and other foodstuffs they were not readily able to identify, ready to be loaded onto horseback. There wasn't much of it, which was another sword in Quintana's side. The ransacking of the Comanche possessions was over quickly and the pile of usable food was pitifully small, but, as Quintana thought, it was better than nothing.

Still fuming over the escape of the Comanche youngster, he turned his attention to the group of Indians now seated, huddled together on the floor.

"Stinkin' savages," he growled, walking slowly around the group. "You, stand up." He pointed at a young girl, perhaps fourteen years of age, maybe younger.

She looked up at him, terrified, unable to understand what he said,

"I SAID ... STAND UP." He shouted, grabbing her by the hair, pulling her roughly to her feet, and dragging her out of the group.

She stood still, trembling, head down, hands clasped together in front of her. Quintana walked slowly around her, appraising.

"This one's not so bad," he said, looking sideways and grinning at the rest of his men, who were standing over the group, rifles in hand. "Let's see what we got heah."

He laid his rifle on the ground, and then reached out with both hands, grasped the edges of the cloth shirt on either side of her neck, and, in one single downward swoop, tore it completely from her body, leaving her standing naked to the waist. Her hands flew to her tiny, barely formed breasts in a vain effort to cover them.

Quintana slapped her face, hard, and smacked her hands away from her chest. When he saw the small buds, his mouth went dry. He licked his lips, and stared at her, wide eyed. She was whimpering with terror.

He took a step closer, grasped the waist of her skirt and ripped it from her; she screamed; he slapped her again; she sobbed quietly as he looked her up and down, and at the cleft between her legs; she was still a child.

"Go get the horses, an' bring mine with ya." Quintana said, looking at the Indians lying dead at his feet. "Let's get this finished and get outa heah."

He looked around about, spotted the dead chief lying crumpled on the floor some fifty yards away, and walked over to him, taking the knife from its sheath as he went.

"Well, now. Ain't you the han'some one?" he said looking down at the painted face. "What's all that mess for anyway?" He waited for an answer, but received none.

"Nothin' to say fo' yourself, huh?" *Wouldn't unnerstand ya anyhow; goddam savage,* he thought, crouching down beside the dead Indian. He reached out with his left hand, grabbed one of the buffalo horns, and dragged the headdress off. *There it is.* He grasped the tip of the braided forelock between two fingers and held it up; it was about eighteen inches long. Then, he dropped it, grabbed it again at the base, pulled hard, and lifted the Indian's head off the ground. He placed the edge of the knife at the base of the forelock where it joined the scalp, and then, with several swift cuts, he sliced away a strip of hair from the front to the back of the skull, leaving the bloody bone exposed. Then he wiped the blade of the knife on the Indian's leather vest, stood, returned the knife to its sheath, and stuffed the bloody lock of hair under his belt, next to that of the girl he had so recently violated.

Thirty minutes later, they had loaded what little food they had been able to find onto their horses and were riding back into the foothills, and were again heading southwest toward Santa Fe.

The sun was going down over the mountains, and Quintana was long gone, when the band of Comanche warriors arrived at the scene of the massacre; there were fifty of them, including the youngster. He had ridden straight to his village to tell of what had happened. The war party was led by a man, a chief, of perhaps fifty, fifty-five years of age. He stood silently looking down at his son, the leader of the slain Indians. His eyes watered. For a long moment he remained, shoulders slumped, face somber, then he turned, stood, rigidly erect, facing the setting sun, his feet wide spread, his arms wide apart over his head, his fists tightly clenched. Then, throwing back his head he howled; a long and mournful wail that echoed across the plain and reverberated around the peaks and bluffs of the foothills.

They gathered the bodies, loaded them gently onto the travois, those that hadn't been destroyed, and the backs of the few ponies they had been able to recover, and slowly, sadly they headed back to their village beyond the foothills to the west.

By midnight, they were home, and the bodies of the dead were already being prepared for their final journey.

The great campfires cast stark, flickering shadows over the sides of the teepees; the steady, throbbing beat of the war drums echoed over the mountains, and the braves, streaked with black war paint, danced and chanted the songs of war, around the fires, watched by their chief, White Eagle, and the rest of the tribal elders.

Chapter 8

April 22, 1865 - Fort Zarah, Kansas

Ignatius O'Sullivan, hat in hand, sat in front of Colonel McGarry's desk. He had arrived at Fort Zarah just in time for breakfast, and, having eaten the first decent meal since dinner at Mother Makepeace's place back in Eureka, was now explaining his mission.

"Confederates?" McGarry looked at him, astounded.

"Captain O'Sullivan," he continued quietly. "The war's over. President Lincoln is dead. It's all over."

"Lincoln is dead" When? How?" The blood had drained from O'Sullivan's face.

"Almost two weeks ago. Assassinated by some no account actor. He expired early on the 10th."

O'Sullivan was lost for words.

McGarry paused for a moment, shook his head and continued, "A week ago, Captain, I lost six men, to the Cheyenne, or so I thought. Now you're telling me that there's a company of Confederate cavalry operating in this area?"

"Cain't say for certain, Colonel. Haven't yet seen hide nor hair of 'em, but I'm bettin' that it was them, an' from what you're tellin' me, I'd say that clinches it. What makes you think it was Cheyenne?"

"They were scalped, Captain, and we recovered two arrows, with Cheyenne markings, feathers."

"Yep, that's it. That's Quintana's mark. He scalps his victims: got my little sister's husband, so he did, an' he violated my sister, too."

"I'm sorry to hear that, Captain. I have not heard from Colonel Richard at Fort Scott, so I had no idea there were Rebs out this way, but now I can understand what you are doing all the way out here. So what's your plan?"

"Well, Colonel, I don't really have anything specific in mind, leastwise not at this point. I have orders to find 'em and bring 'em in, if I can, but I gotta find 'em first, see what we're up against. An' by now I'd say they are probably long gone, out of the territory."

McGarry nodded, then said, "They have not been seen around here, Captain, and I have had patrols out from here almost to Fort Larned, searching for the Cheyenne; no sign of them either. Now, from what you've just told me, I'm not surprised. There's been no hostile Cheyenne activity in this area for more than six months."

O'Sullivan nodded, "They must've turned off the trail, somewhere; headed north or south. I guess the only thing we can do is head back along the trail and look for sign, although it's been more'n a week, an' it's rained, so I very much doubt there'll be anythin' left to find, dammit. Oh... sorry, Colonel; it's the Irish in me, so it is."

McGarry nodded, thoughtfully, then turned to stare at the map on the wall behind his desk.

"I don't know, Captain. As you say, they must have either turned north off the Trail or south. Either way... well, there's nothing: this territory is virtually unexplored." He rose, turned to face the map, and swept the flat of his hand over the lack of detail to the north of the trail. "It's wild country up there; Indian country: Arapahoe, Cheyenne, Pawnee, and a whole litany of others. To the south and west, it's more of the same."

"So I see, Colonel. In which case there's nothin' for it but to return to the scene of the attack on your men an' see what we can find. I have an Osage scout with me. Don't know how good he is, but we'll soon find out, I guess."

McGarry sat down again, shaking his head. He looked at O'Sullivan and said, "I agree, but I don't envy you, Captain. When you leave, I'll send a patrol out with you; they'll guide you to the place where it happened. Is there anything else you need, anything I can do for you?"

"Nothin' more than to replenishing our supplies an' provide us with a good night's rest. The men are tired; been in the saddle for eight days, so they have. Oh, and I need to report to Colonel Richard, so if I could send a telegraph..."

"You'll have what you need, but the nearest telegraph office is in Great Bend, about three miles away. When do you plan to leave?

"Early tomorrow mornin', but not too early. I need to send that wire."

"I can do that for you, Captain. Just write out what needs to be said and I'll have one of my aides ride into Great Bend; it will be in Colonel Richard's hand by noon today. You can use the duty office. I'll pass the word to the sergeant.

"Oh, and before you leave," he continued as O'Sullivan rose from his seat, "Mrs. McGarry and I will expect you and Lieutenant Warwick for dinner this evening; six-thirty, for drinks, dinner at seven."

"Thank you, Colonel. We'll be there." O'Sullivan saluted, turned, and walked out of the office.

It was raining when they assembled the following morning; not just raining, it was a downpour, and windy. It was a little after eight o'clock; Colonel McGarry was waiting, standing outside his office door, under cover of the porch roof, and he had news.

"There's no need for you to backtrack, Captain. I have just received a telegraph from Fort Larned.

"As I pointed out last night, Captain," he began when O'Sullivan joined him on the porch. "Once you travel west, beyond Great Bend, you'll be into some pretty rough country. Fort Larned is your next stop, some thirty miles southwest of here. It's wild country, Captain, Indian country. The fort was established only five years ago to protect travelers on the Santa Fe Trail. It's garrisoned by two regiments of volunteer cavalry under the command of Lieutenant Colonel Jesse

Leavenworth; he also acts as the Kiowa and Comanche Indian agent, and he has his hands full.

"The tribes are at war: the Kiowa, Apaches, Comanche, Arapahoe, Cheyenne, you name it. Well, all that's as it may be, but to cut the story short, Leavenworth has received a communication from Fort Scott, and knows of your mission, and he's expecting to see you.

"But here's the thing: It seems he's been ordered to establish another military outpost some sixty miles to the southwest along the Trail and construction of the new fort, Fort Dodge, is already underway.

"As I said, I received a telegraph from Leavenworth less than thirty minutes ago. He states that his troopers ran into a company of Confederate cavalry, less than a week ago, on the sixteenth. They killed two of them, wounded several more, and ran the rest of them off. Leavenworth said his patrol identified them as a troop of irregular Confederate cavalry, about twenty men. It seems, Captain, that you're on the right track."

O'Sullivan nodded his head.

"Well then, it looks like we've gained seven or eight days on 'em," he said, thoughtfully. "Thirty miles to Fort Larned, you said, Colonel?"

"I did. From here, it's a good day's ride, and another two days from there to Fort Dodge. Well," he said, looking upward into the rain-sodded sky, "it normally would be. In weather like this, though...."

"Yeh, well..." O'Sullivan said, as he looked up at the swirling sea of gray clouds. "Better be on our way, then. Thank you for your help and hospitality, Colonel." He stood to attention, saluted, then turned and walked out from under the porch, and into the rain.

Five minutes later, with each man covered from head to toe in heavy oilskins, O'Sullivan's small force plodded out onto the Santa Fe Trail, heading southwest.

Chapter 9

April 22, Comanche War Party Southwest of Fort Dodge

Chief White Eagle stood by himself on the edge of a bluff high above the foothills that bordered the Cimarron Route of the Santa Fe Trail. For almost two days, he and his war party of fifty-two Comanche warriors, had trailed the white men who had killed his son, his son's wife, and their young daughter. They had not been difficult to find; their trail was well marked and they had found them in the late morning of the first day. For many miles, they followed them at a distance, keeping to the high mountains, watching, waiting. They, the white men, were still in the foothills, heading southwest, following the Great Trail.

The old man stood alone, preferring the solitude of the vast space as he contemplated what must be done. His arms hung loosely by his sides, the leather fringes of his buckskin leggings fluttered in the easterly breeze. To White Eagle, it was more than just a breeze: It was the wind that would carry his loved ones beyond the setting sun to the home of the Great Spirit.

His hair was streaked with gray. His face, heavily lined and streaked with black war paint, was the color and texture of tanned buffalo hide. His chest, also streaked with black paint, was bare, and though there was some loose skin around his armpits, his upper body was tight and muscular.

On his head, he wore the war bonnet of a principle Comanche chief: fifty black-tipped eagle feathers, each crowned with a red plume; the brow band beaded red and black, and adorned with the down of a dozen eagle chicks, also dyed red. Ten thin strips of buckskin, bleached, and then painted black and red, hung from two small, black and red beaded discs, one on either side of the brow band. Other than a knife in a buckskin sheath, and a small, beaded pouch containing eleven .52 caliber paper cartridges, White Eagle was unarmed. His Sharps carbine he had set aside while he spoke to the Great Spirit.

For almost an hour, he stood atop the bluff, his warriors seated astride their ponies some fifty yards away. Finally, he raised his arms, the palms of his hands facing up. He closed his eyes, and tilted his head back to face the sky. For another long moment, he stood there, and then he lowered his arms, turned, and walked swiftly back to join his braves.

With practiced ease, he swung himself up onto the back of his pony. Then he retrieved his carbine from one of his minor chiefs, and, with the barrel of the weapon, pointed along the ridge to the west, kicked his heels into the pony's flanks, and headed at full gallop along the crest of the bluff, following the distant cloud of dust in the foothills below.

Five miles away, Quintana and his men were making their way slowly through the defiles and arroyos in the foothills of a low mountain range that stretched for more than six hundred miles southwest from the Arkansas River to Albuquerque, New Mexico. They would, Quintana knew, have made better going if they had stuck to the well-worn Santa Fe Trail, but that would have exposed them, both to Indians and, perhaps, Federal patrols.

It was not that Quintana was afraid of a fight; he wasn't, but he had always been the one to pick the time and the place, and this wasn't either. Right now, though he was in no real hurry, he had but one goal in mind, and that was the Mexican border, still more than five hundred miles away to the southwest. He had no idea he was being watched.

White Eagle, the warriors of his war party streaming behind him, galloped at full speed along the crest of the bluff. He stopped every now and then to note the position of the white men far below.

It took less than an hour to overtake them, and another thirty minutes before White Eagle was satisfied that he was far enough ahead to execute his plan.

He located the old, well-worn trail down the mountain, a steep and narrow, winding rocky path with room enough for the Indians to descend only in single file, but White Eagle knew the area well, and he knew exactly where he was going.

They left the ponies on top of the bluff and started down the slope. The sure-footed warriors had little trouble negotiating the tight turns and the loose shale underfoot as they moved quickly downhill, until, at last, they arrived at the chief's chosen spot.

Quietly, White Eagle deployed thirty of his warriors in a long line on top of, and behind, a ridge that ranged between fifty and one hundred feet above and parallel to the arroyo along which he knew his enemy must come.

The rest of the war party he placed on a bluff several hundred yards farther to the west. The trail along the arroyo floor made a sharp left turn in front of the bluff, thus effectively creating an impregnable barrier. For the white men, there would be only one way out of the defile, back the way they had come.

White Eagle, now satisfied that all was as it should be, settled down to wait; he did not have to wait for long.

Soon, he heard the ring of steel-shod hooves on the rock floor of the canyon. He listened intently: only one horse. White Eagle was puzzled. There were, he knew, more, many more. As he watched, a single rider dressed in the butternut uniform of a Confederate cavalry trooper rounded a bend and proceeded along the trail toward the bluff upon which he, White Eagle, now lay face down, watching. Then he understood, smiled a tight smile, and nodded his head; this man was a scout. He scrambled backward on his hands and knees, staying well out of sight of the white man on the canyon floor.

White Eagle, reluctant to use his rifle for fear of alerting the rest of Quintana's men, pointed to four of his warriors, then he pointed to the lone rider and made a gesture with his right hand, drawing his forefinger across his throat, a silent order for them to kill him.

Silently, the four warriors rose to a half crouch, fitted arrows to the strings of their bows, took careful aim, and, at another signal from White Eagle, they released them.

Down in the arroyo, the rider never knew what hit him. All four arrows struck him: two of them struck him high on the chest, one in his left arm, and the forth low in his gut, just above the saddle. The force of the impacts threw him backward out of the saddle. The back of his head hit the rocky floor, stunning him; he lay there for several moments gasping, and then ... nothing.

White Eagle smiled grimly, nodded his head in satisfaction, and then settled down again to wait.

Time seemed to stand still as he lay face down on top of the flat rock, the hot sun beating down on his bare back. For a long while, almost an hour, nothing, and then, faintly in the distance, he heard the sound of hooves clicking on the rock floor, and then the muffled sounds of men talking together. He stiffened, looked around, and held up his hand for his warriors to see.

As the guerillas walked their horses into the arroyo, Quintana had an uneasy feeling that they were being watched. It wasn't anything he could put his finger on, just a ... well ... just a feeling. And Quintana had not survived four years of war by ignoring his feelings.

"Whoa," he said, holding up his right hand, and reining his horse to a stop with the other.

"What?" Sergeant Brown asked, pulling his horse to a stop alongside him.

"Not sure." All of his senses were prickling.

For a moment, they sat there, Quintana squinting, shielding his eyes from the sun with his hand, twisting in the saddle, first one way, and then the other, surveying the bluffs and escarpments fifty yards away to either side; nothing! And then, a small stone, more than seventy-five yards away to the front, clicked and fell, starting a small trickle of loose shale.

"GET DOWN. NOW!"

Whooosh. Thud. The steel-tipped arrow hit Brown in the mouth, driving through his teeth, through the back of his throat, and into the base of his skull. Brown's head was thrown back by the force of the impact, and he cartwheeled backward over the horse's rump. Before he had hit the ground, Quintana and the rest of his men had grabbed their rifles and were out of the saddle, taking cover behind the rocks on either side of the arroyo, dozens of arrows clicking and skittering off the stones; the horses were left to fend for themselves.

White Eagle was fuming. The man who caused the pebble to fall would pay dearly for his carelessness.

101

He still held the advantage, though. He had the high ground, and his enemy was outnumbered two-to-one. But, the advantage was a slim one. Other than himself, his warriors were armed only with bows and arrows. Good enough in many cases, as the dead white man on the arroyo floor could attest to, but he well knew that they were armed with quick-shooting rifles. He would have to wait, bide his time, pick them off as opportunities arose. In the meantime, his enemy would suffer under the hot sun.

Quintana, crouched behind a series of large rocks, was wondering what the hell he had run into. Never, since the massacre, now more than seventy miles away, had he seen even a single Indian, not even one, and he had been sure that he had left any pursuit, if there was one, far behind.

Jesus Christ, I sure was wrong 'bout that, he thought, slowly sticking his head up above the top of the rock, trying to look around. *An' where the hell is Pell?* he wondered, thinking about his scout. *Dead, for sure. If not ... I seriously feel sorry for him. Never was one to stand a little pain, was Pell.*

Whooosh. Crack! The arrow slammed into the rock, not more than six inches from the right side of his head. The shaft of the arrow shattered under the impact, the steel head gouged several flat shards of razor sharp shale from the surface of the rock, sending them spinning in every direction, one of them slicing into the back of

Quintana's right hand, leaving a deep, three-inch-long cut.

Goddamn it! Son of a bitch. That was too damn close.

"YOU BOYS KEEP YOUR HEADS DOWN. Y'HEAH?" He yelled, as he dropped back down behind the rock, turned, sat, and leaned his back against it, his rifle on the floor beside him, and sucked on the bleeding cut.

"YOU BOYS, HOLD Y'ALL'S FIRE 'TIL YOU SEE SOMTHIN', THEN MAKE EVERY SHOT COUNT."

He sat, pondering, listening. Nothing. Not a sound. The horses had run back along the arroyo. He checked his weapon: sixteen and one in the chamber. He checked his ammo pouch: full, thirty-five, maybe forty rounds.

He looked to his right: Max Hand and Jed Roker were hunkered down together ten, fifteen yards away. He looked left: Johnny Ike was about ten yards away; Lefty Flint, five or six yards beyond him. The rest, he couldn't see. *They must be on the other side of draw*, he thought, sucking on the back of his hand. He looked at it. *Not so bad as I thought; bleedin's about stopped. Now then, what to do?*

"KEEP A SHARP LOOKOU', BOY'S; SEE IF YA CAN PICK SOME OF 'EM OFF, BUT BE CAREFUL."

White Eagle heard Quintana shouting at his men, but he didn't understand the words, and he didn't care. He knew roughly where each of the remaining seventeen white men were. All he had to do was watch and wait, and as he watched, something caught his eye, something white flashed, just for a moment. He brought the Sharps up to his shoulder, adjusted the rear sight, sighted along the barrel and waited; there it was again; his finger tightened on the trigger; too late, it was gone. He relaxed his finger, but kept watching the same spot, then: BAM!

The heavy rifle slammed back against his bare shoulder, and the distant flash of white disappeared. He lowered the rifle, cranked the lever downward, opening the breach. He reached into the pouch at his waist, removed one of the precious paper cartridges, inserted it into the breach and closed it, cutting open the end of the cartridge and exposing the black powder inside the chamber. He reached into the pouch again, removed a small, copper percussion cap and pressed it onto the nipple with his thumb. Then he pulled the hammer back to full cock, put the weapon to his shoulder, and surveyed the canyon from one end to the other; all was still and quiet.

Holy Sheeit, they got guns, Quintana, thought, still sitting with his back against the rock. He was more than a little disturbed at the revelation. Had he known it was only one rifle, and that its owner had almost no ammunition, he would not have been quite so concerned.

Across the arroyo, almost a hundred yards back down the trail along which Quintana and his men had just come, Corporal Billy Oats was lying flat on his back. He was well out of sight of the surrounding Comanche warriors, but he didn't care, not anymore. He was barely conscious. When White Eagle's heavy, .52 caliber Minié ball slammed into his right shoulder, he had flipped over backward and banged the back of his head hard against the rock floor.

The ball had hit the scapula, almost dead center, and had smashed a hole through it the size of a silver dollar. The wound was mortal, and he was already going into shock.

"FLINT." Quintana shouted. "Come 'ere."

Flint came running, head down so low his nose was almost touching the ground. He fell, breathless, in a heap, beside Quintana.

"I knows what you 'bout to say, Lieutenant, an' I ain't gonna do it," Flint gasped.

"Sure you will, Flinty. We're all dead men if you don't. So, now, or later, I figures it don' matter a whole hill o' beans, but we needs to know what we're up against. An' you can b'lieve me when I tells ya that I don' intend to get ya killed. So, this is what you'll do.

"Far as I can tell. There's quite a bunch of 'em. I spotted bits an' pieces of 'em all along that ridge over there, an' that shot came from down thataway," he pointed down the arroyo to the west. So, I figures there's more of 'em there, up high, in the rocks." He paused for a moment thinking, and then continued: "There ain't none of em behind us, up there," he stared up at the rocky terrain, and pointed. Flint also looked upward.

"How you know that, Lieutenant?

Quintana shrugged his shoulders, "Cain't be. If there wuz, we'd be sittin' heah dead, right now.

"So, Flint. You're gonna head down that way, grab Roker, and then head on up to the top of the bluffs to the rear. When you gets there, you'll toss a pebble down heah, right at m' feet, a *small* one. You toss a rock down an' it hit's me I'll kill your ass. Got it?"

Flint nodded his head.

"Good, you toss the rock, pebble; I'll count up to five, and then I'll yell out for everyone to open fire. When they do, you an' Roker take note o' the reaction from them savages up on the ridges. We needs to know exactly what we're up against. Go now."

Quintana watched as Flint ran, head down to where Roker and Hand were hunkered down. The two talked animatedly for a few seconds, Roker glanced several times at Quintana, who grinned back at him. Finally, the two men slunk off among the rocks, together.

And Quintana waited, and he waited. Then, almost thirty minutes later, "click." A small, round pebble bounced off the rock floor between his feet.

"Yes," he muttered, out loud.

"YOU MEN, LISTEN UP," he shouted.

"Try to keep yo' heads down, but pick a spot where you think you might've seen somethin', somthin' movin', an' when I give the word, you fire one shot at that spot. An' I want every inch o' the ridge, and bluff down there, to the west, covered.

"Ready?" He eased himself into a position where he could see without exposing himself, too much, then counted slowly *one ... two ... three ... four ... five*: "FIRE!"

Fourteen rifles, including Quintana's, spread all around the arroyo, exploded in a rippling ring of gun fire, the noise was deafening. The noise echoed and reverberated around the arroyo.

High on the top of the bluff to the west, White Eagle heard Quintana shouting his orders, but he understood none of it. So he watched, and waited.

Down in the canyon he heard Quintana shout "FIRE!" And then, as the rifles opened fire, he understood. The enemy was trying to draw their fire, find out where they were.

White Eagle jumped to his feet, waved his arms and shouted for his men to stay put. It was a futile effort. All fifty of his warriors let fly with their bows, and were immediately answered by rifle fire.

He watched in horror as five of his braves tipped forward and fell from the ridge.

107

It was quickly over. White Eagle's warriors heard their chief's call to take cover, and they obeyed. Less than thirty seconds after the first round of gunfire, the ridge and the bluff were silent once more; not a single warrior could be seen from the arroyo floor. All, including White Eagle, had taken cover.

"*So there y'are*," Quintana grinned when he spotted the Comanche chief. *An' all dressed up to kill.* The thought had barely entered his mind when the Comanche disappeared behind the rocks.

Quintana's little ruse had worked just as he hoped it would. Not only did he know where the enemy was, he also now knew where the rest of his own men were.

He slid back down, out of sight, and resumed his seat with his back to the rock.

"So," he muttered to himself. "There's a whole bunch of 'em. But we got at least five that I saw, an' maybe more." He looked around. *Where are them boys?* he wondered.

Then, just as the thought passed through his mind, they appeared, running, noses almost to the floor.

"Good work, Flint, Roker. GODDAMN IT!" He shouted, as an arrow hurtled through a gap in the rocks and hit Roker in the chest, the steel tip passing easily through the soft flesh, clipping a rib, and then burying itself deep in his heart. Without a word, Roker slumped down onto his knees, then tipped over onto his back, his knees elevated, feet still flat on the floor, the arrow in his chest sticking straight up.

"Sheeeit, sheeit, sheeit. Goddamn it." Quintana raged.

"Flint. I want that goddam chief. We get 'im, the rest of 'em will run.

"YOU MEN. Listen to me," he shouted. "I'm gonna try an' work around the back of 'em. Y'all gonna keep their heads down. You see anythin' move, shoot it; see anythin' looks like a goddamn feather shoot it; y'all don't see anythin', shoot that, too. Go to it, NOW!"

One by one, the rifles in the arroyo began to fire. Almost immediately, another of Quintana's men on the far side of the trail went down, a ball from White Eagle's Sharps through his neck. He had now lost four of his men, including the scout, Pell; White Eagle had lost seven, including two that were severely wounded.

"Come on, Flint. Show me the way to the top of the ridge."

It took Quintana and Flint some fifteen minutes to make the one hundred-foot climb to the top of the escarpment. All the way up, they slid and stumbled on the loose shale, and the climb was made worse by the need to stay under cover. As they scrambled upward, the men on the arroyo floor maintained a slow and steady rate of fire. Two more of White Eagle's warriors died on the ridge, and another on the bluff where he himself was hidden.

White Eagle was frustrated. He knew that he had his enemy outnumbered more than three-to-one, but the repeating rifles more than evened the odds. He knew that unless he was able to change the situation, he was fighting a losing battle. He had to draw them out into the open, and that was something he knew he could not do here in the mountains; he would have to wait for a better opportunity.

For several moments, he crouched behind the rocks, thinking, unaware that his enemy was working his way along the ridgetop to his right. Then he laid his Sharps aside, cupped both hands around his mouth, waited for a lull in the gunfire, and then uttered several guttural calls that echoed across the canyon.

Satisfied, he picked up the rifle, turned to his left, and ran swiftly and silently, head down, along the bluff, with his warriors following behind. It took less than ten minutes for the rest of the war party to vacate their positions on the rim of the arroyo and regain their ponies on the high bluff to the west; and then they were gone ... but the battle was not yet over.

White Eagle had barely left his position when Quintana and Flint, high on the bluff on the east, found a spot where they had an unobstructed view of the defile. A hundred, or so, feet below, Quintana could see, by the smoke of the rifles, exactly where his men were, and he smiled. *They're doin' one hell of a job keepin' them savages down,* he thought.

Together the two men lay on the rim, and watched, looking for signs of the enemy. Nothing.

"Somethin's wrong, Flint. Where the hell are they?"

As if in answer to the question, a long yodeling call echoed across the mountains.

Quintana and Flint looked up. On the bluff, on the far side of the arroyo, the Comanche war party was riding away at full gallop, heading southwest along the rim, the unknown chief at their head.

"Hah," Quintana said, rising to his feet. "Well bless me, if they ain't cut an' run."

"Guess we whupped 'em, sir," Flint said.

"Not hardly, Flint. That ol' boy's a lot smarter'n I gave him credit for. They don't give up. Not ever. We ain't seen the last of him," he said, watching the cloud of dust on the far side of the arroyo disappearing into the distance.

For a long moment, Quintana stood on the rim, his rifle in his right hand at his side, watching, wondering.

Son-of-a-bitch savages. Goddamn killers, he thought, not seeing the irony in what he was thinking.

"Let's go, Flint. There's no point in tryin' to figure 'em out. We'll find out soon enough, I have no doubt. One thing's for sure, though: we have to get out o' these mountains. They can see us, but we cain't see them.

We're sittin' ducks. We'll find a way outa here and stick to the grassland for a while."

It took the guerillas several hours to find and recapture their horses. By the time Quintana and his men were back in the saddle the sun was already sinking behind the mountains to the west. It was fully dark when they finally reached the edge of the foothills and made their way out into the grasslands.

Quintana was now down to fourteen men, including himself.

Chapter 10

April 24, 1865 - Fort Larned, Kansas

It was not until a little after nine o'clock the following morning that O'Sullivan's troop, soaked to the skin and bedraggled, walked their horses slowly through the gates of Fort Larned.

It was still raining when they arrived. Not the wind-driven downpour they had endured the day before, but a steady, soul-destroying drizzle; cold and miserable.

Rain or not, the fort was bustling. Men were splashing back and forth across the muddy parade ground, smoke was rising from almost every building, and the Union flag was already at the masthead, though it was hanging like a wet rag flat against the pole.

O'Sullivan, Coffin, and Warwick dismounted, leaving Sergeant Holmes to see to the men and horses. Together, the three men walked up the steps and onto the front porch of the command office. When they had stripped themselves of their sodden oilskins, and had draped them over the porch rail to drain, O'Sullivan knocked on the door, pushed it open, and the three men walked inside. The orderly sergeant rose from his desk, saluted and said, with a smile, "Good morning, sir. You must be Captain O'Sullivan. Colonel Leavenworth is expecting you. If you'll give me a moment, I'll let him know you're here."

The sergeant stepped from behind his desk, walked to the rear of the office, knocked on the door, opened it, poked his head inside, and said something that O'Sullivan and the others were unable to hear.

"He'll be just a moment sir," the sergeant said, resuming his seat behind the desk. "If you'd like to sit," he indicated a row of chairs set against the wall, "he's just finishing up some paperwork."

O'Sullivan nodded his head, and the three men sat down. No sooner had they done so when the door opened and a large, jovial man dressed in the uniform of a Lieutenant Colonel appeared; he was smiling broadly. The top of his head was bald and shiny, and he sported a set of whiskers that rivaled O'Sullivan's own.

"Good morning to you, Gentlemen," he boomed. "Lieutenant Colonel Jesse Leavenworth. Expected you yesterday. Won't ask if you had a good journey; can see that you didn't," he said, looking at their water-soaked britches. "Well, never mind; you're here now. Come in, come in. Let's talk. Sergeant Walker," he said to the duty sergeant, "join us, if you please. Take notes."

The four men followed Leavenworth into his office. The three visitors sat down on high-backed chairs arranged in a semi-circle in front of the colonel's desk; O'Sullivan took the center chair, Sergeant Walker sat on a chair set against the rear wall.

"So Gentlemen, I have a busy morning planned, but let's talk first, then you can go get something to eat, and we can meet again later, if need be. But first, Captain, please introduce me to your subordinates."

"My apologies, Colonel: this is Lieutenant Warwick, 14th Kansas Cavalry, and Sergeant Major Boone Coffin."

"Gentlemen," Leavenworth said, nodding his acknowledgement.

"Your mission, as I understand it, is to capture this renegade Confederate unit—well not any more, there is no longer a Confederacy, all but for the final solution of the details. So, what we have here are no more than a gang of outlaws."

He paused, looked at them, nodding his head and smiling.

"So," he continued, "let me give you a little background as to what you're facing. Some of what I'm about to show you, you may already know. Some of it, I'm sure you will not know. Do any of you have experience Indian fighting? No? That's what I thought. Very well, then'"

He rose to his feet and turned to the large map on the wall behind his desk.

"This is the Santa Fe Trail, the Mountain Branch," he said, indicating a thick blue line on the map that ran westward and then southeast from Independence, Missouri, through New Mexico Territory, almost to the Mexican border. "We are here." He pointed to a spot on the map, about mid-way along the line.

"From here, the Trail runs southwest to here, where we're building the new outpost. From there, the old route, the Mountain Branch, heads through the mountains to the west, this way, and then turns northwest through the mountains into Colorado Territory, and then turns again, south through the mountains to Trinidad—coal country. From Trinidad, the Trail turns south again through the Raton Pass, skirting the Sangre de Christo Mountains to the west, to Fort Union, here, and then on to Santa Fe."

He paused for a moment, continued to study the map, then continued, "But that's the long way. This here," he pointed to a second blue line is the Cimarron Route, "it's still the Santa Fe Trail, but it's much shorter, a hundred miles shorter, saves maybe eight, ten days travel. It begins here, just to the west of the new outpost, and runs southwest to rejoin the main Santa Fe, the Mountain Branch, here, just south of Fort Union. The Cimarron Route is quicker, but dangerous, very dangerous: there's little water to be found anywhere, and ... well, as you can see, we are surrounded by Indians, which was the reason for my question.

"There are five, maybe six tribes of Kiowa directly to the south, in this area," he swept his fingers over a large area on the map. In this area, to the southwest, there are at least six tribes of Comanche," again, the sweeping fingers indicated the area. "Apaches here; Arapahoe and Pawnees here, and to the north, and in this area here, there are five tribes of Cheyenne, that we know of."

He paused again, looked seriously at them, "Gentlemen, Federal regulations require that no one, and I do mean no one, is allowed to travel the Trail between here and Santa Fe, on either route, without a military escort; unfortunately ... well, that's not always possible. We do our best to escort all of the stage coaches as far as Santa Fe, and back again, but, with the lack of manpower and such...

"Well, having said that, there's always some crazy loon willing to buck the odds; one or two parties do head out on their own. Usually they sneak away from here under cover of darkness, or they bypass us altogether. When they do ... well, they deserve all they get ... No, no, can't say that. No one deserves what happens to them when those savages get hold of them.

"This is dangerous country, Captain. Why, less than a year ago this very fort was attacked by the Kiowa. They didn't get inside the compound, and we ran 'em off, but they managed to get away with more than a hundred and seventy horses and mules from the coral; bad business," he said, shaking his head.

"Sergeant Walker," he said, looking over O'Sullivan's shoulder. "Please be so good as to fetch me a glass of water."

He waited for the water, gulped most of it down, laid the glass on his desk, and said, "Needed that. Thirsty work, chattering."

He continued, "So let's talk about these outlaws, and where they might, or might not, be. As I have already

117

mentioned, we are engaged in building a new outpost on the Trail, here. It's to be called Fort Dodge." He pointed to a spot on the map to the southwest of Fort Larned.

The ground is already broken and the perimeter walls are going up. I have the Second Cavalry Regiment and the Thirteenth Infantry regiment there, along with a section of the Ninth Wisconsin Light Artillery, two twelve pounders.

"Nine days ago, late in the afternoon of the fifteenth, during a routine patrol south of the new fort, a company of the Second stumbled upon a small force of what they took to be Confederate Cavalry, here." Again he pointed to a spot on the map.

"Knowing that hostilities between the states had ceased, Captain Pearce called out for them to surrender their arms. He was answered by gunfire. During the exchange that followed, Pearce managed to kill two of the outlaws and wound several more before they were able to make their getaway into the mountains, somewhere in this area here." He circled the area on the map with his finger, "Pearce, under orders not to stray more than a half-mile from the Trail, decided not to follow them.

"Now, as you can see, they have several options: They can rejoin the Trail somewhere west of the new fort, and follow the Mountain Branch; they can head southwest through the grasslands, skirting the mountains, or they can turn east, back the way they came. Your thoughts, gentlemen?"

O'Sullivan didn't hesitate, "They're headed for Mexico, Colonel, an' they'll take the Cimarron Route. That's what I would do."

"You're probably right. If so, you have some hard travelling to do. They have a nine-day head start."

O'Sullivan stood and joined Leavenworth at the map.

"What's between here, Fort Dodge, and Santa Fe?" He asked.

"Not much. No settlements to speak of. Too much Indian activity. Just a few stagecoach way stations, all of them well guarded, usually. They'll stay away from those, I think. The stages run quite frequently, and are always accompanied by military escorts.

Once you pass Fort Dodge, you'll be on your own until you reach Santa Fe. Unless you turn northwest, here, and stop by Fort Union, or Las Vegas, here, in New Mexico Territory."

O'Sullivan nodded and contemplated the map for a few seconds, "No. They will stay away from Fort Union ... How far is it from here to Santa Fe, Colonel?"

"Almost five hundred miles. Eighteen, twenty day's ride, if you stay on the Trail. If they are off the Trail— and my bet would be that they are, probably following the foothills, here—and if you follow them, it will take much longer. But, my guess is that you're right. They are heading for Mexico. If so, they'll not go near Santa Fe. They'll cut south, somewhere in this area," he said, pointing to a spot on the map, "close to Las Vegas where the Trail turns to the west, through the mountains, and then they'll head south through the desert and cross into Mexico at, or close to, El Paso.

"We pulled most of our military out of there some six months ago, leaving a skeleton force to provide escorts for the stages and wagon trains, and they'll know that. No, they'll not go near Santa Fe. From here to El Paso, Captain ... it's almost seven hundred miles, maybe more. That's a very long trek, sir."

O'Sullivan nodded, and continued to stare at the map, lost in thought.

"Captain, sir," Warwick said, hesitantly. "If what Colonel Leavenworth says is true, and I don't doubt it for a minute, we are not going to catch them before they reach the Mexican border ... I think it would best if we turned back, returned to Fort Scott ... now, sir."

Coffin snorted, then coughed, but said nothing.

"No, Lieutenant. There will be no turning back." O'Sullivan said, as he continued to study the map.

"You're right, Colonel." O'Sullivan said returning his attention to Leavenworth. "It's exactly what I would do, so it is. I was lookin' to see if there might be a shortcut, an overland route to El Paso, but there's not; leastwise I cain't see one. Other than Las Vegas, here," he pointed to a spot on the map, "an' that's not an option for him, I think, too big of a community, there's nothing but open desert between here an' Mexico. No, they'll stay well to the east of Las Vegas.

"There's nothing else for it," he said, returning to his seat, "we have to go after 'em, and try to catch 'em before they cross the border."

"And what, *Captain*, do we do if they do manage to cross into Mexico?" Warwick asked, his voice was low, but the contempt was unmistakable.

Leavenworth looked at Warwick, surprised at his tone, but he said nothing.

"What do we do, *Lieutenant* Warwick?" O'Sullivan said, his voice ominous and low. "What we do, son, is we go after them, and the consequences be damned. Now, then, if that's not to you're likin', you can pack your bags, get on your bloody horse, and head back to Fort Scott on your own, so you can. There'll be no turnin' back."

Warwick sat bolt upright, stunned at the angry and totally unexpected rebuke.

Coffin coughed again, and covered his mouth in an effort to hide his wide grin.

O'Sullivan turned to face Leavenworth and said, "My apologies, Colonel, but I cannot, will not tolerate such thinkin'"

"Uh ... yes, Captain. However—" He looked hard at Warwick, seemed about to say something, then changed his mind. "Apology accepted, sir, although none was needed." He glanced again at Warwick, then quickly looked away; Warwick's face had turned bright red.

"Thank you, sir," O'Sullivan beamed benignly at the colonel, and continued, "Now, if the weather breaks, we can make thirty miles a day, maybe a little more. We've already made up almost a week on 'em, an' I'm bettin', they don't know we're after 'em. If that's so, they won't be runnin'. If they're followin' the mountains, they'll make fifteen, maybe twenty miles a day. We should be able to catch 'em by the time they make it all the way to here." He pointed to a spot on the map just to the north of El Paso.

"Colonel, what supplies can you let me have?

"Anything you need, Captain. Make a list and give it to Sergeant Walker. He will see to it. When do you intend to leave?"

"First thing in the morning; no point in dilly dallying. The new fort is how far, Colonel?"

"Sixty miles, and I agree; the faster you get on their trail, the better. In the meantime, I suggest that you and your men get cleaned up, eat a couple of good meals; they'll probably be the last you'll see for a couple of months; and get some rest, you're going to need it."

The three men left Leavenworth to start his day. As they stepped out into the rain, O'Sullivan turned to Coffin and said, "Of you go, me old son. Go see to the mounts. I'll catch up with you at breakfast."

Coffin and Warwick turned and started to walk away.

"Just a moment, Lieutenant."

Warwick turned and walked the couple of steps back to O'Sullivan. Coffin did not look back, he continued to walk away, a slight smile on his face.

O'Sullivan put his left arm around the young man's shoulder, "Now see here, boyo. It may be that I was a wee bit outa line in there, an' if I was, I's sorry for it, so I am. But, here's the thing, old son: jumped up non-com, so I may be, but I'm still your commandin' officer.'

"Now then, Dil," Warwick looked perplexed at O'Sullivan's use of his first name, "it wasn't what you said in there that I object to—I'm always open to suggestions—it was how you said it that I didn't like. My sergeant major caught it, an' I know damn well the colonel did, too.

"You might be one of West Point's finest, an' I'm sure that y'are, but I have four years o' bloody combat under me belt, an' I seen things, and I done things that you'll never even dream of.

"So here it is, me young lad: I'm real easy to get along with, just ask Coffin. That bein' so, you can say anythin' you like to me, an' you can suggest anythin' you like, just so long as you do it respectfully. I will not put you down for that, no I won't. In return, I'll treat you like the smart young officer that y'are. An' from here on in, there'll be no more of your uppityness, or your

123

sarcasm and innuendo. We have tough times ahead of us, real tough times, so you an' me have to get along together. I have to be able to rely on you ... without reservation. Agreed?

Warwick, unable to hide his shame, simply nodded his head.

"Good lad. Now let's put all this unpleasantness behind us. We'll make a new start, so we will. Yes?"

"Yes, sir."

"Good. Off you go then I'll join you in the mess in a minute, or two an' we'll eat a steak for breakfast, my treat. Grab Coffin an' tell him to join us; we need to talk about what's ahead an' what supplies we need."

By eight o'clock the following morning, the troop was mounted and ready to leave Fort Larned. The rain had stopped and the sun was already rising over the peaks and ridges to the east.

O'Sullivan had explained to them what was ahead. One of the three pack mules had been loaded with two casks and six spare canteens of fresh drinking water. Added to that, each man carried two canteens. They had stocked up on food for the men and feed for the horses, and they had an extra hundred rounds of ammunition per man. It had been O'Sullivan's thought to request that he be issued with some artillery, perhaps a mountain howitzer, but he gave up the idea when Warwick reminded him, respectfully, that they were probably headed into the mountains, and the heavy gun would be more hindrance than asset.

They were ready go.

O'Sullivan offered his thanks to Colonel Leavenworth, handed him a communication for telegraph to Colonel Richard explaining his intentions, and said goodbye.

He affectionately rubbed Lightning's velvety muzzle, fed him a carrot, checked the horse's leathers once more, and then swung himself easily up into the saddle.

"Captain," Leavenworth said, looking up at him, "a quick word before you go, if you don't mind."

O'Sullivan nodded, and dismounted.

"I asked you yesterday if you had any experience with Indians," he began. "You haven't, so I will offer a little advice. They will be watching you; they always are, take my word for it. You must keep your wits about you at all times; be constantly on the lookout for them; you can be certain they will be there, somewhere. Watch for smoke on the mountain tops; it's how they communicate.

"You are a small party—tempting; they want guns. If they think they can take you by surprise, they'll try it. But, bad as they want guns, they also know they can't win against them in a stand-up fight but they are masters of guerilla warfare. Stay on the trail, if you can. If not ... well, I wish you good fortune, Captain."

The two men saluted each other, and O'Sullivan remounted.

"Forwaaard, ho!"

The gates swung open, and, with a salute and a wave, he led the troop at a fast canter out onto the Santa Fe Trail. The gap between him and the Confederate guerillas was now a little more than a hundred and seventy miles.

Chapter 11

April 25, The Grasslands

Quintana was right. White Eagle had no intention of giving up his quest for revenge. Staying atop the bluffs and plateaus, he followed the Confederates, keeping pace with them, watching, waiting. And he made no attempt to hide his presence. Time and again, Quintana, or one of his men, would spot a lone warrior high on the ridge in the foothills, watching. Sometimes it was the chief himself; the brilliant colors of his headdress leaving no doubt as to who it was, and the constant vigil from above made them all nervous.

For almost three days, they skirted the foothills, heading southwest. The terrain was rough, the going slow: an amalgam of shale-strewn desert, tall grass, rocks and saguaro, with no end in sight. They were able to maintain no more than walking speed. By nightfall they were camped out in the open, close to the edge of the foothills, a little more than thirty-five miles from the arroyo where the battle had taken place.

All through the long days, the sun beat mercilessly down of them; the nights, in stark contrast, were cold, the silence broken only by the sounds of the creatures of the darkness: the screech of an owl, the incessant drone of grasshoppers and cicadas, the bark of a prairie dog, the mournful howl of a distant coyote. *Prairie dog? Coyote?*

"Flinty," Quintana said, shivering. "Fire ain't gonna last but another hour, an' I need it to last 'til mornin'. Take three men an' go find some firewood."

Flint, holding his hands to the flames, looked up and across the fire at Quintana, and he was not happy; he was afraid of the dark, and even more afraid of what he thought might out there, waiting for him. He did, however, know better than to argue, and he rose, reluctantly to his feet.

"Max, Johnny, Lefty" Flint said, pulling his Colt Army and checking the loads. "Let's go."

It was no more than fifteen minutes later that the three men returned, dragging several large chunks of dead wood, mostly branches of desert willow.

"We gotta do somethin' about them Indians," Quintana said, once the fire was blazing, and his men had settled down. "We'll soon be needin' water, an' that means we need to be back in the mountains, but that ain't gonna happen 'less we get rid o' them savages."

"You got a plan, Lieutenant?" Flint asked.

"Ain't but one thing we can do, an' that's go find that son-of-a-bitch chief an' kill him."

"How we gonna do that?"

"Well, he ain't gonna come to us, that's for sure, not unless he thinks he can catch us unawares. So, we'll just have to go after him."

He reached inside his jacket and withdrew a large, battered silver pocket watch, flipped it open, held it up to the light of the flames, and squinted. It was a little before ten o'clock.

"Here's what we'll do. Last time we saw that son-of-a-bitch was just before sundown, when we was setting camp. He thinks we're down for the night, an' that means he probably is too. I picked this spot 'cause it's close to that draw over there," he pointed in the direction of the shadowy outline against the night sky. "I figure there's a way up onto the ridge. We'll leave the horses heah an' go find 'em; kill as many as we can, an' their damn horses, too. If we can kill the chief, so much the better; if not, well they cain't follow us on foot."

He paused and looked at his men as they warmed themselves around the fire. They were all nodding. It was a good plan, and they were happy to be doing something, anything.

"Good! Now, check your weapons. Make sure your six-shooters are fully loaded with one under the hammer, an' a full seventeen in your carbines. We ain't gonna have no time to reload, and we ain't gonna be able to see to do it anyways. When we find 'em, no one shoots until I do, an' then, by God, you shoot sure an' slow; you make every shot count, you heah?"

He looked at each of them in turn, questioningly. He received a nod from each in return.

"Good! Now check the horses, put em that side o' the fire so they can be seen, so them savages will think we're still here, bedded down, an' load up the fire. Then we'll go get that son-of-a-bitch." He looked upward at the quarter moon, *Hope to hell there's enough light to see our way up there.*

Ten minutes later, on foot, in single file, the thirteen men left their camp, trotting quickly toward the draw, the fire crackling merrily, throwing sparks high into the air.

As they began their climb upward, Quintana stopped and looked back at the campsite, now more than a hundred and fifty yards away. Against the flickering blaze he could see, as he knew he would, the silhouettes of the horses, and he grinned. *That should do it. Now you son-of-a-bitch, it's my turn.*

It was well past midnight when they reached the top of the mountain. The climb up the loose and rocky slopes, in almost complete darkness, had taken them more than two hours. When they finally clambered over the crest and onto the top of the bluff, they were exhausted. For ten minutes, they lay on their backs recovering their breath, until, at last, Quintana was ready to move on.

He raised himself onto his elbows, looked around, and said, "We'll go south. They ain't gonna be ahead of us, leastwise, I don't think so. Come on, get up."

Silently, bent over at the waist, their heads down, they ran in single file along the rim of the bluff. They hadn't gone far, when Quintana held out his arm, a silent signal for them to stop.

"Look," he whispered, pointing. "See, over that way."

In the distance, well away from the rim of the bluffs, there was a red glow.

"Campfires," Quintana said, he could barely be heard. "It's them. Quietly now, follow me. Any man makes a sound, I'll cut his throat. Got it?"

No one answered, but they all got the message and, silently, they crept forward.

The Comanche were camped in a depression surrounded by desert willow trees and juniper. There were two guards posted, one on either side of the encampment. The ponies were tethered to trees on the far side. The campfire was large, but now no more than a huge heap of glowing embers that crackled and snapped. There was enough light from the fire for Quintana to be able to assess the situation: aside from the two sentries, all of the Indians were sleeping, wrapped in blankets, lying on the slopes of the depression around the fire.

He crept back to his men and, in a low whisper, outlined his plan. "Far as I can tell," he began, "there're two sentries: one on this side an' one on the far side. The rest of 'em are scattered around a big ol' hole in the ground. The horses are tethered on the far side, just to the right. They are our primary objective. If we leave any of them savages alive, and there are horses, they will keep after us: no horses, no pursuit.

So, here's how we do it: I'll take the sentry on this side; You, Flint, take the sentry on the far side. You be ready, an' when I shoot, you shoot. We'll split into three sections," he continued. "You three will circle to the left, you three to the right, the rest, you an' Flint are with me. My group will concentrate on killin' the horses; the other two groups will concentrate their fire on the Indians; kill as many of 'em as you can. We ready?"

They were.

"Good! Now, go. Spread out; make not a damn sound. Nobody, an' I mean NOBODY," he hissed, "takes a shot until they heah me shoot first."

The three groups split up, one going west, another to the east, and the rest, with Quintana, crept slowly through the night until they were within fifty feet of the nearest sentry.

Quintana adjusted his position until he had a clear view of both the sentries and the tethered ponies. The nearest sentry was a dark silhouette against the flickering flames; the second, and the ponies, were easily visible in the firelight.

Quintana looked at Flint, nodded his head, and raised the Henry rifle to his shoulder; Flint did the same.

BAM, BAM! The quiet of the night was shattered as the two rifles fired, almost together. The head of the sentry closest to them seemed to expand as a cloud black mist against the firelight spread outward when the heavy ball hit it. The second sentry keeled over backward and lay still.

Instantly, as the rifles of the center group opened up on the ponies, the sleeping Indians leaped to their feet, looking wildly around, grabbing for their weapons. As they did so, the other two groups also opened fire, with devastating effect. Six went down under the first volley. White Eagle, now on his feet, but crouched down behind the fire, lance in hand, howled something Quintana's men heard but could not understand. Then he rose slightly with the lance in his right hand. He drew it back at waist level, and with a mighty twist of his upper body, brought his arm and the lance forward in a long, powerful, sweeping underarm throw. The lance arched upward, its long steel tip flashing in the firelight.

Fifty feet away, Private Flint was taking careful aim at the head of one of the wildly bucking ponies. As he squeezed the trigger, something in his peripheral vision caught his eye. For a second, he held his fire and glanced sideways. All he saw was something, no more than a dark blur against the sky, hurtling downward toward him.

The war lance struck Flint high on his left shoulder and drove downward, the twelve-inch long, steel spear point plunging down through flesh and bone. The impact hurled him backward, the rifle spun from his fingers, and pinned him to the dirt floor.

"Goddam," Quintana shouted, looking down at him, then looking wildly around the seething camp. "WHERE ARE YOU, YOU SON-OF-A-BITCH?" he yelled at the top of his voice. But White Eagle was gone, away among the shadows. His men—what was left of them—had followed him in response to his call, most of their weapons left behind, as they ran swiftly through the night, away from the carnage.

It was over in less than ten minutes; to Quintana it seemed like an hour, but he had achieved his objective, and at the cost of only one man, Private Flint; the Comanche were gone.

"CEASE FIRE! RALLY TO ME!"

He stood, walked forward into the camp, rifle at the ready, his men on either side of him, and he looked around. He spotted a warrior, squirming on the ground, blood pouring from a gunshot wound in his lower chest.

With one hand, Quintana pointed the rifle at the Indians head and pulled the trigger; the man jerked once, and then lay still.

"You two ... go make sure all of the horses are dead," he said, still staring down at the dead Indian. There were a half-dozen loud reports, and the two men returned.

"All dead, Lieutenant."

Quintana nodded his head, and then walked slowly around the camp, counting as he went.

"Eleven," he said. "We only got eleven of 'em. An' we didn't get the chief, leastwise, I don't think so." He said, picking up White Eagle's war bonnet. Then he shook his head in frustration, and said angrily, "They'll be back. Burn everything. Leave nothing they can use."

They gathered everything they could find: bows, arrows, lances, clothing, food, blankets, and threw it all on the fire. Quintana watched, staring silently into the blaze, thinking.

"Hey," he shouted to one of his men who was about to throw a bundle of arrows into the fire, "Gimme those; we might need 'em later."

Then he tossed White Eagle's war bonnet into the flames; the feathers flared, and in less than a moment it was no more.

He looked around once more, making sure that they had missed nothing, and then said, "Let's go." He turned from the fire and walked away into the darkness, his men following in single file. As they passed by Flint, the feathered lance still protruding from his shoulder, Quintana stopped for a moment and looked down at him. The man was breathing raggedly, but unconscious. Without a word, Quintana jacked a cartridge into the chamber of his rifle, pointed it at his head, and then said, "Sorry, Flinty. Cain't leave you here for them savages to find, an' I cain't take you with me, so—" And he pulled the trigger. Flint didn't feel a thing.

An hour later, White Eagle and his men crept silently back into the camp. The flickering flames of the fire turned his already dark features, now twisted with a raging anger, into a blood red mask. He walked slowly around the camp and stood for a moment staring at the massed bodies of almost fifty ponies, and eleven of his warriors. Silently he walked past the dead sentry, until he came to where Flint was lying on his back, the war lance sticking almost straight upright. He kicked him, nothing, the man was dead. He grasped the shaft of the lance, put his left foot on Flint's chest, and pulled, working the lance back and forth to free it from the bone. It came free, and White Eagle wiped the blood from the point on Flint's shirt. Then, with a jerk of his head, he indicated for his men to follow him.

Thirty minutes later he was standing on the rim of the bluff, his warriors in a group, several yards to the rear. Far below, out in the grasslands, he could see the glow of Quintana's campfire.

He flipped the lance around in his hand and slammed the point into the dirt at his side. Then, his feet wide apart, his arms in the air, he threw back his head and let out a long wailing call.

Quintana, now almost a mile away at the bottom of the mountains, on the edge of the grasslands, heard the call. He stopped dead in his track, shivered, turned around and looked up at the rim. Faintly, by the light of the quarter moon, he could see the outline of the Indian chief.

"Hah," he said, to himself. Then he turned again and continued on into the night. A little after three o'clock in the morning, they had broken camp and were once again heading southwest toward Mexico. He was down to just twelve men, including himself.

White Eagle, now on foot and without weapons, other than his war lance, had no option but to turn northeast and trudge back to his village, his loved ones unavenged.

Chapter 12

April 25, Fort Dodge

The sixty-mile ride from Fort Larned to the new Fort Dodge took less than a day and a half; they rode in through the makeshift wooden gates at just after eleven-thirty in the morning dusty, hungry, and tired.

Captain Henry Pearce, the officer commanding the new post, having been called to the dirt wall by a sentry was waiting for them.

"Captain O'Sullivan," Pearce said, as O'Sullivan dismounted. "I heard you were on your way. Good journey?"

"Long, very long, Captain."

"Well, Captain. I have little to offer in the way of luxuries, but what I do have, you are welcome to. How long do you plan to stay here?"

"Long enough to rest the horses, and the men. We'll be on our way early tomorrow morning."

"Very well, I'll have tents raised for you and the lieutenant?"

"Yes, Captain, I thank, you. The sergeant major and the rest will do for themselves. In the meantime, we need to talk, if you have time to spare."

"That I do. Not much going on here; at least not yet. The perimeter is fairly secure, but ... well, you never know. There are a lot of hostiles out there, and it wouldn't be the first time ... well, enough of that. Let's get some coffee and sit down."

"If you don't mind, Captain, I'd like Lieutenant Warwick and Sergeant Major Coffin to attend: one, they need to know what's going on, and two," he looked hard at Warwick, then winked at Coffin, "I value their input."

Coffin grinned, but said nothing; Warwick looked a little nonplussed, but he too said nothing.

"So, Captain," Pearce said, as the four of them drew small folding stools into a group in front of the large tent that Pearce was using as his field headquarters, "tell me about this Quintana."

"I don't know that much about him. What I do know is that he is, was, one of Quantrill's men, and so were the animals he has with him. He's brutal, ruthless, and a stone cold killer. It's entirely possible he is responsible for the massacre of a Union cavalry patrol east of Fort Zarah two weeks ago. Now the war's about over, he seems to be headed off on his own, on his way to Mexico, so we think. No matter, he's no more than a common outlaw, an' we have to get him."

"Yes, I heard about the incident at Fort Zarah; bad business."

"But you had a run in with him down here, did you not, Captain?"

"True; can't say for sure it was him, but the two men we killed were wearing what might once have been Confederate uniforms."

"Tell me about it, if you please, Captain."

"There's not much to tell, Captain. The whole thing lasted no more than a few minutes."

O'Sullivan, Coffin, and Warwick listened intently as Pearce described his encounter with the guerillas.

"How many were they, sir?" Coffin asked, when Pearce had finished his narrative.

"Not sure. More than twenty ... twenty five or six, I should guess. Less the two we killed, maybe twenty four, or five. Then again, I would say even less than that; they lost a couple more at least. My men were certain they wounded at least two."

"Yeh, an' knowin' what we know, Quintana would not want to be slowed by his wounded..."

Pearce nodded in agreement, "Poor bastards are probably lying out there somewhere, vultures would clean 'em up as quick as you please."

For another hour, the four men sat together, chatting, mostly about the war and what the surrender of Lee, and now the likelihood that Johnston was about to do the same, would mean for the future, and in particular their careers. Finally, allowing that none of their speculations were going to matter a tinker's cuss for the outcome of whatever might lie ahead, O'Sullivan rose to his feet, tossed the dregs of his coffee into the dust, and said, "Right oh, then, we'll see to our needs, and be on out first thing in the morning, if that's alright with you, Captain Pearce."

"Of course, but before you go, let me say this: I will escort you to the place where were encountered these ... these ... ruffians. Might save you an hour, or so, of searching. Also, we butchered one of those early this morning," he pointed to a small heard of longhorns in a pen at a corner of the perimeter dirt wall. "Steaks for dinner? The three of you. Six o'clock. I'll also have meals served to the rest of your men. Agreed?" he asked with a smile.

"That it is, Captain. That it is," O'Sullivan said, nodding his head enthusiastically, and with an even bigger smile than Pearce.

"And a couple more things, Captain." O'Sullivan said. "We have food enough for perhaps a week, but water ... well, if we could top off our casks and canteens? And if you could authorize your blacksmiths to check our animals, and make any necessary repairs to hooves and shoes; God only knows when we'll get another chance."

"I'll have my men see to it for you. Six o'clock then," he said, offering his hand first to O'Sullivan and then to Coffin and Warwick.

It was just after first light the following morning, April 27, that O'Sullivan and his small troop, along with Captain Pearce and a sixteen-man patrol, rode out of Fort Dodge, heading due west, past the long abandoned Forts Atkinson and Mann and then southwest along the Cimarron Route of the Santa Fe Trail.

141

By seven-thirty that morning, they had arrived at the spot where Pearce had encountered the Confederate guerillas. A few minutes later, they were close to the place where Quintana had turned off the Trail and had headed for the mountains. Even though Pearce remembered the encounter vividly, he was unable to pinpoint the spot precisely; Big Man, the Osage scout, however, had no trouble finding it.

He walked his horse slowly along the Trail, at the head of the column, scouring the rocky shale for signs. After just a few minutes, he uttered a small, guttural sound at the back of his throat, turned, and pointed, indicating a spot some eight or ten yards off the Trail, then he swept his finger upward and pointed off into the distance at the mountains to the west.

O'Sullivan, Pearce, and Warwick stood at his side, Coffin and Holmes just to the rear of him, they all gazed out over the desert grasslands; O'Sullivan was shaking his head.

"It's been ten days, Captain," O'Sullivan said to Pearce as he continued to stare off into the distance. "How far ahead can they be? I wonder."

"Hard to say. The going in those mountains ain't easy. Hundred an' fifty miles, maybe."

"Ain't goin' to be easy for us either."

"Nope, but here's what I would do, if I were in your place—if you're interested, that is."

"Of course. What *would* you do?"

"I would not go into the mountains at all. Well, not until I had to, to find water, maybe. I'd cut southwest and skirt the foothills, you're not going to miss him; he's too far ahead. I'd make best speed, considering the conditions southwest through the grasslands, an' I'd use him," he said nodding toward the Osage. "I'd send him on ahead, on his own, into the foothills; yes, the foothills. If he wanted to go the Mountain Route, he would have done so. The high mountains west of the foothills are not easily accessible. So, he has no pack animals, leastways I didn't see any, an' that means he's going to need water, and that's available nowhere except ... the foothills.

"You can make twenty five miles a day, maybe more, if you stay in the grasslands. If he continues doin' what he's doin', you'll catch him before he crosses the Cimarron River into New Mexico."

"That, my old friend, sounds like a plan." O'Sullivan thought for a moment, looked around at Coffin, his eyebrows raised in question, and received a nod of Coffin's head in return.

"Well then, Captain, the grasslands it will be. I thank you, Henry." He held out his hand to Pearce who took and shook it warmly.

"You're welcome, Captain. I wish you good fortune, and may God be with you."

"Oh he is, Henry, he is."

The two men parted company. Pearce turned back toward Fort Dodge, and O'Sullivan turned west off the Trail headed toward the distant mountains.

What he didn't know was that Quintana was now barely one hundred miles ahead, this due to his slow progress through the foothills, and his several skirmishes with the Comanche.

Even though the desert grassland floor was anything but smooth, they were able to make good speed. At a slow trot, they were to cover the four miles to the edge of the foothills in just under an hour. There, O'Sullivan called a halt and they took the obligatory ten-minute break to rest and water the horses; the ten minutes turned into more than twenty as they discussed their options.

Finally, O'Sullivan sent Big Man to follow Quintana's trail into the foothills. He was to follow the trail until he was sure of Quintana's, intentions, then, in order to maintain the pace, he would rejoin O'Sullivan.

O'Sullivan watched Big Man as he disappeared into the mountains, and then resumed the chase, heading southwest through the grassland, skirting the foothills: the pace was a steady, slow trot; with breaks, they were making a little more than five miles every hour: thirty miles in a seven-hour day.

By nightfall, Big Man had rejoined the troop, and they were almost forty miles to the southwest of Fort Dodge and were now slightly less than a hundred miles behind Quintana.

The night air was crisp and O'Sullivan's men were grateful for the warmth of the campfire. Big Man, during his sojourn into the mountains, had killed a young white tail deer. On his return to the group, he skinned and dressed it. Soon the mouthwatering aroma of meat roasting over an open fire permeated the small camp. At that moment, even for O'Sullivan, life was good.

O'Sullivan and Warwick sat together several feet back from the fire; the scout, Big Man, was seated several yards away to O'Sullivan's right. Coffin was at the spit, carving the roasted flesh with a large Bowie knife. The rest of the troop was sitting together in a group on the opposite side of the fire.

O'Sullivan took the thick slice of meat that Coffin cut for him, tossed the scalding hunk back and forth, from one hand to the other, cooling it. He took a bite; the juices ran from the corners of his mouth, and he leaned quickly forward to save his uniform. Coffin poured coffee for the three of them, then sat down on a log to Warwick's left. For several moments, they sat quietly eating; the fire snapping and crackling, sending showers of sparks whirling up into the sky as the juices from the roasting meat fell into the embers.

"I wonder how far ahead they are," O'Sullivan mumbled, his mouth full of food.

"Ufff!" Coffin grunted through his food.

Warwick smiled, but said nothing.

"Damn, that was good," O'Sullivan smacked his lips and threw a chunk of gristle into the fire. Then he stood, drew his own knife, a cut another thick sliver from the haunch, and then returned to his seat.

A couple of minutes later, he threw the remains of his food into the flames, sending more sparks skyward, then he rose, walked twenty yards, or so, into the darkness and relieved himself.

"So," he said, returning to his seat, "I wonder where they are, how far away, an' what they're doin'."

"The same as us, I shouldn't wonder," Coffin said, cradling his tin mug full of coffee. "How far ahead? Ain't no tellin'."

"Hey, Big Man," O'Sullivan said, turning to look at him. "What do the signs say? How far ahead are they?

The Osage thought for a moment, then said, "Four, five days, maybe."

"Naw!" Warwick said, skeptically.

The Osage shrugged his shoulders, but didn't reply.

"That close?" O'Sullivan asked, also doubtful.

"Not close. Long way. But we faster, if he stay in mountains."

O'Sullivan turned back to the fire, picked up a long stick and idly poked at the embers.

"Look, sir," Warwick said, quietly, "I mean no disrespect, but do you have any kind of a plan for when we catch up with them?"

O'Sullivan smiled as he looked at the young lieutenant. "That I do, lad, that I do."

"And?"

"An' what?" Again, O'Sullivan grinned at him.

"Dammit, sir. What's your plan?"

"You tell him, Boone."

"I'd say, Lieutenant," Coffin said, quietly, "that the captain's plan is to kill every last one of 'em."

O'Sullivan nodded his head.

"That's your plan? Christ. Oh, um, sorry, Captain, no disrespect, sir," he stammered, looking worriedly at O'Sullivan.

"None taken, son," O'Sullivan said with a smile. "West Point, right?"

Warwick nodded his head.

"Where did you finish?"

"Twenty out of forty two. Last year."

"Humm, mid-way; not too bad," O'Sullivan mused. "So tell me, son, have you seen any action?"

"No, sir. I came straight to Fort Scott from West Point."

"I figured as much. There's no flint inside you, yet; just insecurity. Oh, simmer down, son. That's not an insult, just an observation. The flint only comes from experience under fire."

Warwick relaxed.

"It'll come, so it will. Always does. Eh, Boone?"

The sergeant major nodded in agreement.

"You—You—" Warwick began to speak again, then hesitated, and closed his mouth.

"Out with it, son. There ain't no fool questions, 'cept those you don't ask?

"Wasn't nothing, sir. I was just wondering ... well, about what action you've seen; you and the sergeant major, but..."

"Too much, son. More than a man can tolerate, normally, but war does strange things to a man, so it does. But ... well, you just does what you have to do, an' you either get through it or ... well. An' some that do get through it, might just as well not have; aside from the devastatin' physical wounds—lost arms, legs, sight— there's what war can do to a man's mind. Turns 'em into jelly fish, many of 'em.

"We was at Shiloh, Boone an' me, an' then that little piece of hell that was Stones River. We both went with Colonel Streight 'cross Northern Alabama; almost never made it through that one, but we did, didn't we, me old friend?" He looked at Coffin, who smiled slightly, dropped his head to stare down at the floor between his boots.

"And then there was Franklin ... Aw hell, that's enough of such foolishness," he interrupted himself. "It's all over now, so it is; at least they say it is ... All over except for this little mess, an' we're about to clear that up, too."

For several moments, the three men sat together in silence, staring into the flames, O'Sullivan idly stirring the embers with his stick, thinking ... thinking. Finally, he seemed to gather himself together, sat upright, and said, "Get some sleep, boys. We'll get an early start in the morning. Let's go get the son-of-a-bitch an' end this."

But Quintana wasn't in the mountains. He was heading southwest through the grassland, and he too was making good time, almost matching O'Sullivan's thirty-five miles per day.

Chapter 13

April 27, Cimarron Grasslands, Kansas

By noon the following day, O'Sullivan and his troop were some sixty-five miles, as the crow flies, to the southwest of Fort Dodge, skirting the foothills of the mountains: Big Man was more than a mile ahead of them.

O'Sullivan was a little surprised when the Osage came galloping back toward them.

The scout reined in his horse in front of the two officers, turned in the saddle and pointed back the way he had come. "You come, quick. Something bad happened!" Then he spun his horse and, at the gallop, headed back through the grasslands from whence he had come, O'Sullivan and his men followed.

They rode for more than a mile, until, at last, Big Man held up his hand and brought the column to a halt.

"See, there." He pointed to a spot some fifty yards ahead.

"What?" O'Sullivan asked. "I don't see a thing ... wait, oh yes I do. What's that?" He pointed to several sticks of wood, barely visible above the long grass. He nudged Lightning's flanks gently with his spurs, and walked him slowly forward; Big Man was close behind, followed by Warwick and Coffin.

"Indian?" O'Sullivan asked, looking down at the brightly painted poles.

"Comanche," Big Man replied. They were looking at the remains of a travois. "Something very bad happen here. Come see"

He walked his horse a little farther on, then pointed at several spots on the ground.

"Much blood." He swept his arm, pointing with his forefinger, in a wide circle. "Many die here. See?" He leapt down out of the saddle and picked up a piece of dark cloth, made even darker by the dried stains.

"This girl child's shirt; this blood."

"How do you know it belonged to a girl, Big Man?" Coffin asked.

"Small. For child. Boys not wear anything; chest bare, always. Girls cover all." He walked a few feet farther on, then stooped again, and picked up another bloodstained shirt. "This one, woman's.

"White man do this ... six, maybe seven days. They kill many. All, I think. Thirty ... forty, maybe more. Much blood; all over." Again he pointed, describing a wide circle with his finger.

"Quintana!" O'Sullivan growled.

"You sure it was white men that did this?"

"Only white man use steel on horse's feet. Comanche, no!"

"Had to be Quintana, then. What happened to the bodies?"

"Comanche come for them. Large number."

"O'Sullivan, felt the hair on the back of his neck begin to prickle, and looked nervously around, over the grasslands to the mountains beyond. Nothing.

Big Man smiled, a rare thing. "You not worry, Captain," he said, swinging himself back up onto his horse's back. "Comanche gone; long time; five, six days.

"Maybe you need search no more. Comanche will find these white men, and then—" He drew the forefinger of his right hand across his throat.

"So you say, me old china; so you say. Can you tell which way they went, the white men?"

"That way." Big man pointed to the foothills.

"You go on ahead, then. Stay close enough that we can find you. Don't want to get lost up there."

"You not get lost; I find you." The Osage wheeled his horse and headed off toward the hills at a gallop.

O'Sullivan and his men watched as he disappeared into the distance.

"Bedad, this is a wicked man, so he is, if what Big Man says is true."

"Typical Rebel scum," Warwick muttered.

"Scum? This one? Yes, but they ain't all like him. Most of 'em are no different than you, an' me, an' Coffin here. But this one, yes, this one is different.

Well, there's no point sittin' here on our asses, dreamin' about him. Let's go get the son-of-a-bitch."

152

He twitched the reins to the right, and nudged his flank; Lightning responded and they headed off after the Osage at a swift canter.

Quintana, having decided to stay out of the mountains, and put as much distance as possible between himself and any possible pursuit by the Comanche, had maintained a steady but grueling pace throughout the day. By nightfall, they had traveled more than forty miles and were approaching the border of the New Mexico Territory, and the Cimarron River just beyond.

Around six o'clock in the early evening, he called a hold and ordered the men to camp for the night. He figured he was, by now, well beyond the reaches of any pursuit, Indian or Federal, but he was not happy. His troop had been reduced almost by half, and God alone knew what lay ahead, the border still more than five hundred miles away.

And so he sat alone on the far side of the camp fire, away from the rest of his men, under a rapidly darkening sky, thinking, gnawing on the leg of a roasted jack rabbit one of his men had managed to shoot, sucking noisily on the bones,.

Goddamn savages, he thought. *Eleven good men gone, 'specially Brown ... an' Lefty Flint.* He tossed what was left of the rabbit into the fire, and lay back on the ground, his hands behind his head, his head on his saddle, and stared up into the sky, a bluc-black ocean showing just an early scattering of the brightest stars.

I guess we can take it a little easier from here on. Cain't be no more'n twenty-five, thirty miles from the Cimarron. Should be able to make it that far by t'morrow, all bein' well. We need food an' water...

He was asleep before the quarter moon rose in the eastern sky.

As Quintana and his men were bedding down for the night, O'Sullivan and his men, slightly more than a hundred miles away to the northeast, were also looking for a safe place to bed down for the night, and O'Sullivan, was not at all comfortable with his surroundings, having taken Pearce's warnings to heart.

When they had reached the foothills some three hours earlier, they found Big Man waiting for them.

"They go that way," he said, pointing to the southwest. "They follow trail between rocks. I go, you follow. You find place to camp. I find you."

"Er ... an' what about them Comanche?" O'Sullivan asked.

Big smiled, shaking his head. "No Comanche. I go. You follow; find place to camp. I come back, along trail, this way." He turned and rode away.

"Alright, boys. You heard what he said. Let's find a nice safe place, if there is such a thing."

An hour later, as the sun dipped down behind the mountains to the west, they found themselves at the entrance to a small box canyon. The opening into the canyon was perhaps forty feet wide; from there it opened up to form a closed gorge some sixty feet wide by a hundred feet deep; the walls of the canyon towered vertically upward more than two hundred feet.

"Holy Mary," O'Sullivan said gazing up at the walls of the canyon as they filed slowly inside. "This is either the safest place on earth to make camp, or it's the worst."

"Hell of a good spot for an ambush," Coffin said, also gazing up at the rim. "They catch us in here, we're all dead."

"Well, we ain't found anywhere else, an' it'll soon be dark. So this has to be it. Organize a fire, Sergeant Major. You, young sir," he said to Warwick, "you come with me.

The two officers turned and left the canyon, turned right again, and followed the trail for several hundred yards.

"What did you think of that back there?" O'Sullivan asked.

"What, the canyon? Safe enough for now, I guess."

"No, no! Not the bloody canyon, that mess out on the prairie, where Quintana killed all of them Indians."

"There's not much to think, Captain. If he did it, and I can see no other solution, he's a goddamn maniac. What kind of man murders innocent women and children? Christ."

"The same kind that murdered them folks back in Elbow, an' raped my kid sister," he said, the anger simmering inside him.

"They have to be stopped, Lieutenant. They ain't soldiers; never was; just bandits, plain an' simple. They took advantage of the war, put on gray uniforms, an' raped, killed an' stole across five states. Now the war's over, they'll just keep on rapin' an' killin', unless someone stops 'em; might as well be us."

"Captain," Warwick said, quietly. "I need to say something..."

"Well, son, get on with it."

"I want to apologize for my earlier behavior."

"Stop it, son. Ain't no need. We finished with all that days ago, back at Fort Larned. An' anyways, I know what I am. No spit an' polish here. You're right, I ain't no gentleman, not officer material."

"Sir, I don't think that's quite true." Warwick said, shaking his head; he looked pale in the waning evening light.

"Yeh, it is so true, an' when this mission is done, if I'm still alive, I plan to leave the army. I done more'n me share, so I have. It's time for me to go, but not before I get Quintana. He has to pay for his many sins, so he does. Come on, let's go back."

"Ho, Captain." The shout echoed through the mountains. O'Sullivan looked back up the trail. Big Man was trotting along toward them.

"Have you found anything?" O'Sullivan asked as the scout drew near.

"They passed this way five days ago; no more. If Comanche find them first..."

"If the Comanche find them first, Big Man, the Comanche will be in big trouble. Do they have guns?"

"Few guns. Bow, lance, knife."

"Yeh, well Quintana an' his bunch have modern repeatin' rifles. The Comanche with their bows an' lances will be no match for them."

"Haha!" It was a short, sharp laugh, derisive. "You, Captain, do not know Comanche. They warriors. They not care about guns. Quintana will not know they are there until too late."

O'Sullivan, stared at the scout, half convinced, then he shook his head and said, "If you say so, ol' son; if you say so."

He looked up at the darkening sky. "Let's go get something to eat, while we can still. Come on, Lightin' me ol' friend." He gave the horse an affectionate slap on the neck, and nudged him with his spurs. The great horse whickered, nodded his head, and clattered slowly back along the trail and into the box canyon where a campfire was already blazing. The air was filled with the aroma of boiling coffee. The remains of yesterday's deer were already on a makeshift spit being turned slowly by one of the troopers.

The sun rose early the next morning, at least that's how it seemed to O'Sullivan, but in actuality, it was their elevated position and vast flatlands to the east that created the illusion.

By seven o'clock, they had breakfasted, the fire had been put out, the horses rubbed down and saddled, and the pack animals were loaded, and they were out of the box canyon and headed southwest, onward and upward through the foothills.

The morning air was clear and crisp, there was not a cloud to mar the vast reaches of cobalt blue sky that stretched endlessly toward the far horizon and the half disc of the sun still not yet fully risen above it. It was one of those rare mornings, when it felt good just to be alive, to feel the cold air permeate through the sinuses, and the cool mountain breeze against the skin.

Even the animals could feel it. They lifted their hooves just a little bit higher, their ears were pricked, and their muscles rippled as they navigated the narrow, rock-strewn trail.

The air among the men was one of expectancy. Big Man had left a half-hour earlier; the rest of the troop followed in single file, O'Sullivan leading, closely followed by Warwick and Coffin.

All morning long, they made steady though slow progress through the foothills while Big Man followed Quintana's trail. They stopped, more from habit than adherence to army regulations, ten minutes in every hour to rest and water the horses. At ten o'clock, they took a thirty-minute break, made coffee, checked the horses shoes and leathers, and then were soon back in the saddle.

The terrain was stark, a mixture of red sandstone and tan-colored limestone topped with stands of juniper and prickly pear; the skyline punctuated by the silhouettes of giant saguaro.

By noon, the sun had almost reached its zenith, and its blistering rays reflected downward from the near vertical escarpment that bordered the trail to the right, searing the eyeballs of man and beast alike. By one o'clock in the afternoon, the temperature had risen into the nineties; the early morning breeze was no more; the rocks and boulders shimmered in the relentless heat.

O'Sullivan had called a halt for the sixth time since they had left the box canyon some seven hours earlier. They were in a shady spot under the lee of an overhanging bluff. It was cooler, but not by much. He ordered the saddles and packs removed, and the animals watered, fed and rubbed down. That all done, they sat down on their saddles, in a long line, their backs against the face of a cliff, and tried to rest.

Their reverie didn't last long. The sound of steel-shod hooves on rock to the west brought them instantly alert, reaching for weapons.

Two minutes later, Big Man clattered around the bend, spotted them, reined in his horse, and in one fluid movement dismounted.

"Comanche find Quintana," he said to O'Sullivan with a jerk of his head to indicate the direction from which he had just come.

"The Comanche? Where? Is he dead?"

"Not know. One hour from here. You come."

"Boots an' Saddles," he said with a sigh, but loud enough for all to hear. "Boots an' saddles." Twenty minutes later, they were mounted and back on the trail following the Osage scout.

It was a little after three o'clock in the afternoon when they reached the scene of Quintana's battle with White Eagle; Sergeant Brown's body—what was left of it—still lay at the side of the trail. A short distance farther on, the body of Quintana's scout still lay on its back, the four arrows pointing skyward.

O'Sullivan halted the column and ordered the men to dismount. While they waited, he, the Osage, Warwick, Coffin, and Sergeant Holmes stood in a circle around Brown's body, silent and thoughtful.

Warwick shuddered at the sight of the arrow sticking out of what was left of his face; the wild animals had not been kind to Brown's remains, and the body was already in a state of advanced putrefaction; the stench was nauseating. Warwick felt the bile rise into the back of his throat, he swallowed hard, but maintained his composure.

After a moment or two, O'Sullivan, without a word, turned and walked the few yards to where the body of the scout lay, and the other four men followed.

"Bedad, the poor fella never knew what hit him", he said, staring down at the arrows, and the animal-ravaged face.

He reached down, grasped the arrow that protruded from the dead scout's gut and pulled. It came away easily, the putrefied flesh sucking on the shaft, gas escaping from the body cavity with a sound not unlike a gasp, and the stench it produced was almost palpable, thick enough to cut with a knife.

Warwick's stomach was no match for this, and he turned quickly away, staggered into the rocks and threw up, coughing, choking, and spluttering.

O'Sullivan and Coffin watched in amusement. "You done, son?" O'Sullivan asked, quietly, so that the rest men waiting farther back down the trail couldn't hear him. "If so, come on back. This is somethin' you'll need to get used to, an' quickly; leastwise, I hope you will."

Warwick returned, looking a little sheepish, wiping his mouth on his sleeve, his eyes watering from his violent efforts to empty his stomach.

"It's alright, son," he said, clapping him gently on the shoulder. "First time's tough for everyone, an' this ... well, this is ... tougher than most, so it is, but you'll be fine. Just breathe deep and give it a moment."

O'Sullivan stepped away from the body, gestured for Big Man to follow him, walked a few yards farther on along the trail, then stopped and said, "Are there any more?"

The Osage nodded, "One there," he pointed to where Corporal Oats' body lay hidden among the rocks. "One there," He pointed on along the trail to the spot where Private Roker's body still lay, also hidden among the rocks and boulders.

"Any Comanche?"

The Osage nodded his head, "Some, I think. Blood over there. No bodies. Comanche take them to village for journey to the home of Great Spirit."

O'Sullivan nodded his head, seemingly lost in thought. Then he shrugged his shoulders, turned and walked quickly back to the main group, gesturing for Coffin and the other three men to follow him.

"So," he began, addressing the group, "we need to know what has happened here, an' what exactly we are up against. Big Man, I need you to go up onto the ridge and see what you can find, an' then up onto that bluff," he pointed to the spot White Eagle had occupied only four days earlier. "An' Big Man, we need to know about any Indian activity, now an' in the past; we get caught down here we're all dead. An' I want to know where they all went, an' how many. Take your time; get it right."

He looked around at Sergeant Brown's body, shook his head and said, "You four men," he pointed to them in turn, "see what you can do about burying the bodies; ain't right to leave 'em just lyin' here. If nothin' else, pile some rocks on 'em, cover 'em up."

He then designated four more men to handle the horses and mules, and then set the rest to searching the arroyo: the rocks, clefts and ravines.

They discovered no more bodies; the Comanche had indeed, as the Osage had said, removed their dead, although the rocks and canyon floor below the ridge still bore the signs of where they had laid: great patches of dried blood turned dark brown by the sun.

It was almost two hours later, just after five o'clock in the afternoon, when O'Sullivan decided that enough was enough. He called his men together again. Big Man had already returned from the crest of the plateau; the canyon was all in shadow, the sun having disappeared behind the escarpment, the towering cliffs no more than a hundred feet to west of the trail.

"We need to get out of this canyon," O'Sullivan said, looking nervously up at the rim. "We cain't stay down here. Them Comanche will pick us off one by one. He turned and looked at the Osage scout, his eyebrows raised, the question unspoken.

"No Comanche, Captain. They gone ... four days. That way." He pointed to rim, and then to the southwest.

"What about Quintana?"

"Gone too. That way," again he pointed; this time at the top of the ridge to the east. "They leave canyon."

"Show me," he said, mounting his horse. "MOUNT UP. Let's go."

The Osage also mounted and the troop cantered southwest along the canyon. A half-mile farther on, the Osage reined in his horse, turned to face the troop, and pointed to a narrow gap between the rocks on the left side of the trail.

"This way," he said, and, turning again, he urged his reluctant mount through the gap; O'Sullivan, did the same, followed by the rest of troop in single file.

The narrow path ascended gently for several hundred yards, then angled sharply to the right, widened appreciably, angled back to the left, and sloped gently down through the foothills to a great plain below.

It was already dark when they finally reached the grasslands. But there was no stopping, at least for a while; O'Sullivan wanted to put some distance between them and the mountains.

When he did finally call a halt, the moon, now almost half-full, was already high in the sky to the east; queen of the great star field, queen of the night.

O'Sullivan and his men had been in the saddle, or at least on the move, for more than thirteen hours. They were tired, hungry, and miserable, but the day was not yet over; the horses and mules had to be cared for, fed, and watered, a fire had to be built, and the men had to eat.

It was well after midnight when O'Sullivan, Coffin, and Warwick were finally able to wrap themselves in their blankets and lie down to sleep. But sleep did not come easily to any of them; and for Warwick, the hours until daylight were spent tossing and turning on the hard ground, the horrific images of what he had seen in the arroyo turned into a nightmare that ended only when O'Sullivan shook him awake at first light.

While O'Sullivan and his men slept that night, April 28, Quintana also slept, just ninety-five miles away to the southwest on the banks of Cimarron River.

The gap was closing.

Chapter 14

April 29, McNees' Crossing, Cimarron River

Quintana and his men crossed into New Mexico, and over the Cimarron River, just after noon on April 29, and there, they set up camp on the southern banks of the river. It was a good spot; the river was less than a hundred feet across, the water crystal clear, fast-flowing, and bordered to the east by vast tracts of grasslands and prairie, and by high mountains to the west. The water level was low for this time of year, the dry wash on either side extended from the water's edge for another thirty feet or more.

It was an area of great natural beauty—deceptively beautiful. Almost forty years earlier, in 1828, two scouts working for a wagon train traveling to Santa Fe rode out to check the river crossing. All was quiet, so the two men, John McNees and Daniel Munroe, decided to take a short break. They dismounted, tethered their horses to a nearby tree, and lay down in the shade. Sometime during the next half-hour, or so, they were attacked by Comanches. John McNees was killed on the spot; Munroe was wounded but managed to escape; he died several days later. McNees was buried near the crossing, which was named after him.

But Quintana didn't know any of this, and was in a relaxed and expansive mood: the weather was fine, the crossing was uninhabited, the Comanche—as far as he

166

could tell—were no longer a threat, the fish and game were plentiful, and he planned to spend a couple of days resting the men and horses, and himself.

As soon as they had made camp, Quintana stripped off his clothes and walked naked into the fast-flowing icy waters of the Cimarron. The water at the middle of the river was, perhaps, three feet deep. He sat down on the shale riverbed; the water came up to his neck, and he reveled in it as it rushed by, creating an eddy around his neck that splashed now and again over his head. He sat for a long time, twenty minutes or more, absently rubbing his arms and legs with the palms of his hands, thinking.

The future was a mystery, a timeline he'd thought little about, that, as he sat thinking, ended just beyond the Mexican border south of El Paso in Juarez. How long till they crossed, he had no real idea. What he did know was that El Paso was still more than four hundred miles away.

Too far, he thought. *Too damn far to sit around idling the goddamn time away.* It was right then that he made up his mind, or rather he changed it. *Need to keep movin'*

With new resolve, he rose to his feet and splashed through the water and out of the river. The campground was less than a hundred feet from the riverbank and, by the time he reached the fire, he was shivering from the cold.

For several minutes, he stood in front of the fire, close to the flames, then he dressed himself, and called the men together.

"Listen up," he said. "The plans changed. We'll spend the rest of the day here, an' the night, but I want to be away early in the mornin'. We have a long way still to go, an' you never can tell what might be round the next corner, or the one previous, so we need to keep movin'.

"Max, take two men and see if you can rustle up some game; might as well get a good meal while we're here. Ikey, you an' Booger see if you can catch some fish. Y'all" he looked at both groups of designated hunters and then continued, "get as much as you can, but be back before dark. What we don't eat tonight, we'll take with us. You, you, an' you, go fill all the canteens; God only knows when we'll find more water.

"Proust, you head out back down the trail, see if we're bein' followed. Gould, you go south, see what lies ahead. Go to it; everybody back here before dark, no later."

The hunting went well, the fishing did not

Young Johnny Ike and Booger Whitlock had headed upstream in search of fish with little thought about how they might catch said fish, should they find them; they had left camp carrying only their rifles. They hadn't been gone very long when: Bam, Bam, Bam.

The sound of rifle fire upriver brought every man left in camp leaping to his feet and grabbing for weapons.

"Get down, take cover," Quintana yelled, diving for the shelter of a fallen tree trunk.

They lay there, for several minutes, tense, waiting, then: Bam, Bam, Bam ... Bam, Bam.

"What the hell," Quintana jumped to his feet. "With me," he shouted as he ran through the undergrowth, head down, toward the sound of the gunfire.

For a quarter mile, they ran, following the bend in the river, then: Bam, Bam. They saw them, knee-deep in the middle of the river, rifles at their shoulders pointing down in the water: Bam ... Bam. The water splashed upward from the impact of the Minié balls.

"Goddam it," Quintana yelled, at the top of his voice as he walked out of the undergrowth to the riverbank. "What the hell are you doin'?"

The two men, startled, turned around, swinging their rifles. Quintana and his men ducked their heads in alarm.

"Hey, Lieutenant," Ike shouted, lowering his rifle, a wide grin on his face. "We's fishin', just like you said."

"Goddam it, you crazy sons-o-bitches. I thought we were bein' attacked. Get the hell outa there and back to camp afore I put a ball up your asses. Go now," Bam, Bam, Bam. The Minié balls from Quintana's rifle slammed into the water between their legs, showering them with water. "Go on, git!"

The two men ran to the riverbank, water splashing, soaking them. Quintana's men, standing behind him, watching, were laughing uncontrollably; Quintana looked around at them, scowling; he did not see anything funny. The men immediately wiped the smiles off their faces.

The hunters returned just as the sun was setting, turning the sky above the mountains deep red, and the saguaro on the ridges into stark, black silhouettes. They brought with them a half-dozen jackrabbits, two prairie dogs, and a white-tail deer: food enough to last for several days, at least.

They were up well before dawn the following day; the upper rim of the sun's disk was barely peeping over the horizon when they rode out of camp.

Seventy five miles away to the northeast, Captain O'Sullivan was also making ready to leave camp. His afternoon by the river at McNees' Crossing had cut Quintana's lead by ten miles.

O'Sullivan arrived at Quintana's camp in the grasslands east of the mountains and White Eagle's camp at around three o'clock in the afternoon of May 1. Big Man was nowhere to be seen.

It wasn't until a little before four o'clock that the scout came riding at full gallop from the direction of what appeared to be a narrow cleft in the foothills of the mountains.

He reined in his horse, leaped down, and joined O'Sullivan, Coffin, and Warwick seated by the now blazing campfire.

"You come," He said to the captain and pointed toward the mountain.

"Why? It looks to me that they went that way," he replied, indicating the direction he believed Quintana had taken with a jerk of his head.

"Yes. That way, but you need to see. Come." He walked the few steps to where his horse was standing and swung himself up onto its back, and then he sat there, watching O'Sullivan; he wasn't the only one: Coffin and Warwick were looking quizzically at him too.

With a heavy sigh, he threw the stick he'd been poking the fire with onto the ground and rose to his feet.

"Righty ho, then; let's go take a look; Lieutenant, Sergeant Major. You're with me. The rest of you, see what you can do about getting us something to eat."

The three men quickly saddled their horses, and mule, and mounted.

"Away you go, then; lead on," O'Sullivan said. The scout nodded, kicked his horse into action, and cantered away toward the draw, some quarter mile from the camp; O'Sullivan, Warwick, and Coffin followed close behind.

Half way up the mountain, they had to dismount and continue the last hundred yards, or so on foot; the narrow trail having turned into an almost vertical footpath, strewn with loose rocks and shale that made the climb up to the rim arduous and tiring. Fifteen minutes later, they staggered over the crest and onto the flatland. The three soldiers were breathing hard; the Osage, breathing normally, stood with his hands on his hips smiling, waiting.

"This way," he said, pointing. "See?'

In the distance, above a stand of juniper and desert willow trees, fifty or more black shapes circled slowly.

"Vultures," Coffin said.

The Osage nodded, and set off toward the circling birds at a slow, loping run.

"Holy Mother," O'Sullivan gasped, as they approached the trees. "What's that bloody awful smell? Oh m'God."

Big Man nodded his head, and said, "Come, see."

As they approached White Eagle's abandoned campsite, the all-encompassing smell of rotting flesh grew even worse. The three men pulled their bandanas up over their mouths and noses in a vain attempt to block the stench, but it was useless; soon all three were retching, trying to hold what was left of the mid-day meal in their stomachs. For Warwick it was a vain attempt, even before they reached the pile of dead Indian ponies, he was heaving his innards out onto the floor between his feet; O'Sullivan and Coffin were little better off; the Osage was little bothered by what confronted them.

"What the hell happened here?" O'Sullivan muttered, gazing at the putrefying mass of bodies. "There must forty of fifty horses there."

The scout nodded his head and said, "Quintana."

The dead ponies were littered over an area some sixty feet in diameter. Their bodies had been ravaged over several days by wild animals and scavenging birds and were a mass of open decaying wounds: entrails lay in piles beside open bowels and other cavities; flies and maggots infested every opening, and the stink was unimaginable. Dozens of huge black vultures were hopping around on top of the bodies, pecking, tearing away chunks of rotting flesh. It was a sight that none of them would ever forget.

They did not see Flint's body. What little there was left of it was scattered over a wide area, the bones picked clean.

"Oh, bejesus. I can stand no more of this. Let's get outa here."

Back at the footpath that would take them back down to the grasslands, O'Sullivan called a halt. "For the rest of me days, I'll never be able to forget that, so I won't," he said, sitting down on a rock on the edge of the bluff. "Never in all me days have I ever seen the likes of it, not outside of a battlefield, an' that's no lie."

"The man is a maniac, Captain," Coffin said, sitting down beside him; Warwick also sat.

"No. The man's no maniac; Crazy maybe, but cunning ... wiley. He knew he couldn't beat 'em, so he stopped 'em the only way he knew how: kill as many as possible, and kill all the horses. That way they couldn't follow him. He's long gone now, an' so are the Comanches, walkin' home, I shouldn't wonder."

He turned to look up at Big Man who was standing behind him, his arms folded over his chest, gazing out over the grasslands far below.

"How many Comanche did he kill? Can you tell?"

The scout shook his head, and said, "Some, not many. Not much blood. He drive them away; burn weapons," he said as he reached down and handed O'Sullivan a half-dozen, fire-blackened steel arrowheads.

"Oh, yeh," O'Sullivan frowned, pursed his lips, then continued. "No weapons, no ponies, no pursuit. Oh yeh; this man is good, very good.

"How long ago, Big Man?"

"Four days. No more."

O'Sullivan nodded, gazing out over the great plain below, thinking.

"So, we're gaining on him." He jumped to his feet, a new light in his eyes. "Let's go. Get some rest. I want to be away before sunup tomorrow."

It was just after five-thirty the following morning when they broke camp and headed southwest; Quintana and his men would not mount up for another hour.

The gap was now less than ninety miles.

Chapter 15

May 1, Beckler's Station, 55 miles Southwest of McNees' Crossing

The ride from McNees' Crossing on April 30 was relatively easy and uneventful, and Quintana and his men made good time. By nightfall, they had covered almost forty miles and were camped on the banks of a small creek, but all was not well. The relentless pace was beginning to tell, not just on the men, but more so on the horses. Several were limping, and all of them were showing signs of malnutrition.

Quintana was no stranger to this section of New Mexico, having ranged far and wide during the war under the command the Confederate guerilla leader, William Quantrill. He knew exactly where he was, and he also knew there was a stagecoach station on the Santa Fe Trail, now some twenty miles to the east. He knew, too, that the station would have fresh horses on hand, and supplies.

His plan was to rest overnight, rise early the following morning, and ride east across the desert, join the Trail, find the station and resupply his command with fresh horses, food, and water.

They rose just as the first beams of sunlight appeared over the horizon to the east. There was only time for coffee before they were in the saddle and riding east toward the Santa Fe Trail.

They reached the Trail at a little after eight-thirty and turned southwest; Beckler's Station was just four miles away.

Beckler's Station was an important stop along the Santa Fe Trail, not just for the stage lines, but also for the wagon trains that were headed to and from Santa Fe. Thus, it was a relatively large compound with a perimeter fence, a store, and a coral, wherein were held some sixty-plus horses, all of them belonging to one stage company or another. There were also eight men living on site; hard men, men used to life on the Trail. Their payroll was split between Mr. Beckler and the stage lines; their job was to defend the station from marauding Indians. They were not, however, prepared for what was about to befall them.

Crandon Beckler was in his mid-sixties; his wife, Elsie, was two years younger; they had no children. The two had owned the station for more than twenty-five years. Over those years, he had seen sights that no man should ever see. He was a hard man, and his time in the wilderness was almost done—so he thought. It was time to sell and move on, spend what time he had left with his wife of forty years, in relative luxury, perhaps in Santa Fe.

As the station came into view in the distance, Quintana slowed the troop to a walk. One of the eight guards was on lookout on a tall wooden tower fifty yards away from the front of the store.

It was no surprise to Beckler, or his wife, when Quintana and his men rode up to the front of the store at a little after nine o'clock that morning, May 1. He noted the gray uniforms, but they didn't bother him, nor did they bother the guard up on the tower; in fact, he waved a welcome to the column, then settled back down in his chair, and pulled his hat down over his eyes. The war, after all, was over, and they were not the first ex-Confederate soldiers that had visited the station.

"Booger, you're with me," he said as he dismounted. "The rest of you stay heah; keep a sharp lookout."

The two men walked into the store, their boot heels thumping on the wooden planks.

"Howdy, gents," Beckler said, affably. "What kin I do for you?"

"Howdy y'self," Quintana said, equally affably as he drew his Colt Navy revolver and shot Beckler in the chest. The gunshot reverberated around the inside of the store. Beckler, his mouth wide open in shock, sank slowly to the floor.

On hearing the gunshot, Elsie Beckler, who had been tidying one of the back rooms, ran into the store and was confronted by the widely grinning Quintana who, before she could utter a word or a scream, shot her too.

Outside, on hearing the gunfire inside the store, the guard on the tower jumped to his feet and grabbed his rifle; before he could raise it to his shoulder, however,

178

Johnny Ike brought him tumbling down from the tower with a ball in his chest. Even as he hit the ground, the other seven guards came running from the various buildings around the store; three came running from the left, and four from the right. Some already had weapons in hand, some pulled pistols from their holsters as they ran. They were met by a fusillade of rifle fire from the still mounted Confederate guerillas. They fell, all of them, tumbling and spinning, until, at last, they lay still on the dusty ground, blood seeping into the dust around them. It was over in a minute. The sounds of the gunfire echoed away into nothing, wafting over the far reaches of the plains beyond the station. All were dead; Quintana had not lost a single man.

Quintana, now in no hurry, walked slowly around the store, taking inventory. He stopped for a moment, looked down at Elsie Beckler, licked his lips, and then moved on.

"Booger, go get four men. Drag them two out into the open," he said, nodding at the bodies of Beckler and his wife. "Lay 'em out on the porch, on their backs. Then I want food, all you can find; an' cartridges for the Henry's; leave the rest of the rifle ammo. Grab the rest of the pistol cartridges, too." Quintana said as he took two boxes of .36 caliber shells from the shelf behind the counter, and tipped them into the cartridge box on his belt.

Outside, he ordered his men to dismount and remove the saddles and packs from their horses' backs.

"Pick you out some new mounts, boys," he shouted, gesturing toward the corral. "I wanna be away from here no more than an hour from now; go to it."

Quintana pulled the saddle from his own horse, threw it down on the wooden porch in front of the store, and then removed his saddlebags, blanket, and the bundle of arrows he had taken from White Eagle's camp, and threw them down beside the saddle.

He slapped his horse's rump, sending it cantering away, then headed for the compound where his men were busy catching their horses. For a moment or two, he stood with one foot on the lower rail, his chin rested on both of his arms that were folded on the top rail. He smiled to himself when he saw the youngster, Johnny Ike, manhandling an unruly beast, trying to drag the unruly animal over to the gate in the fence, the horse resisting with his front hooves jammed solidly into the dirt.

Quintana climbed over the fence and walked quickly to where Ike was still struggling, hauling on the halter rope.

"Give him here, boy," he said, taking hold of the rope. "Go find yourself another. One a little bit more your size. This one will suit me just fine."

Ike did as he was told. Quintana stepped close to the big horses head, whispered something in its ear and then turned and walked toward the gate, the big horse nodding its head, followed meekly behind.

"When you're done," he shouted back over his shoulder, "turn all the rest loose, an' then collect all of the guns that're lying around the compound; throw 'em down the well, along with any that're left in the store."

Back at the storefront, he gently saddled the big horse, all the time talking quietly to it, and then he flipped the reins over the hitching rail, reached down and picked up the bundle of arrows. One by one, he walked to each of the corpses, pushing an arrow into each of the gunshot wounds.

"Damn, I hate them Comanches," he said to himself, grinning widely. "Now look what they done."

By eleven o'clock, they were all mounted on fresh horses, their supplies securely fasted to four packhorses, and they were on their way west, back toward the mountains some twenty miles away.

By seven o'clock that evening, May 1, night was closing in over the desert; Quintana, within a half-mile of the mountains, had turned southwest once more, and was camped for the night. The gap was still about eighty-five miles: four days.

O'Sullivan spent the night of May 1 at Quintana's camp thirty miles northeast of McNees' Crossing. By five-thirty the following morning, he was back on the trail, and by one-o'clock on the afternoon of May 2 he had arrived at the Cimarron River crossing.

With at least six hours of daylight left, he decided to take no more time at the river than to water and rest the horses. Two hours after his arrival, at three o'clock, he ordered the animals saddled and loaded and had resumed the chase. The signs were sparse and far apart; the going was slow. By sundown, he had made only another twelve miles and had camped for the night.

By seven-thirty the following morning, they were back in the saddle and headed southwest, still finding sign in the sparse desert, but making slow progress. They arrived at Quintana's camp from the evening of May 1 late in the afternoon. O'Sullivan was not happy with the day's progress, but due to the fact that signs were hard to find, even for the Osage, and in deference to the welfare of his animals, he decided to make camp and rest them for as long as possible; he didn't resume the chase until nine o'clock the following morning, May 4.

Quintana had increased his lead by more than ten miles.

Chapter 16
May 4, Beckler's Station

Although O'Sullivan had risen early the morning of May 4, he was in no hurry to get moving. They were tired, worn out, men and horses alike. They had been on Quintana's trail for more than twenty-five days and had covered almost six hundred miles. It was time to take it easy, at least for a little while.

Although they were still in camp, the day had started, as it always did, at around sunup. The men were soon up and about; the fire stirred and rekindled, coffee, bacon, and beans were cooking, the horses and pack animals were being fed, rubbed down, readied for another long day.

O'Sullivan, Coffin, and Warwick were seated together on their saddles beside the fire. They wore blankets around their shoulders, cradling tin mugs of scalding coffee; the early morning air was chill, the sky a vast expanse of deep purple, the glow of the coming dawn just showing on the horizon to the east.

"Where's Big Man" Warwick asked, looking around, not seeing the Osage scout.

He's been gone a while," Coffin said. "He left on foot almost an hour ago, that way." He indicated the direction in which the scout had left with a nod of his head, his mug held close to his lips as he inhaled the steam.

"Lookin' for sign, I shouldn't wonder," O'Sullivan said, thoughtfully.

"How much longer, do you think, before we find him?" Warwick asked.

"No idea. We're gaining on him, but slow," the captain said, "Still more'n four hundred miles to the border, an' we have the advantage."

"How so?"

Coffin looked at Warwick and smiled, but said nothing.

"He don't know we're after him." O'Sullivan said. "That's how so."

Warwick nodded, remained silent for a moment, then said, "You know, Captain, I'm wondering how he's keeping going. Our animals are suffering, and his can't be doing any better, worse in fact. At least, you'd think so, wouldn't you?

O'Sullivan nodded, and said, "True enough, son. That's been on my mind too. We've been babying our beasts, never more than a slow trot, and they are, were, all in the best of health when we started out, so they were, but still..."

Just then, Big Man appeared out of the gloom, startling the men by the fire.

"Sign," he said, pointing east toward the dawn. "He go that way."

"You sure, Big Man?" O'Sullivan asked, frowning. "He's been headed southwest along the edge of the

184

foothills for more than two hundred an' fifty miles. Why would he change now? The Santa Fe Trail is that way, right?"

The Indian nodded, and said. "He go that way, for sure; sign not lie." He pointed again toward the sunrise. "Trail that way, ten, twelve miles, no more."

"When?

"Three, maybe four days."

O'Sullivan nodded, looked round at the men still busy with the animals, and said, "Get some coffee and something to eat, Big Man. We'll not leave for a while yet."

The sun was fairly high in the eastern sky when O'Sullivan's small troop finally left camp and followed Quintana's trail east.

An hour and a half later, they reached the Sanata Fe Trail and he called a halt.

"Which way, Big Man?"

The Indian dismounted, walked across the trail, stooped and studied the ground on the far side, then he rose, walked a short way along the trail to the southwest, then back, and walked a few yards to the northeast, then returned to the column waiting on the western side of the Trail.

"Not sure," he said, shaking his head. "Much sign, many horses, wagons. This way, that way," he pointed along the trail first one way and then the other.

"Not go that way." He pointed across the Trail to the east. "No sign!"

O'Sullivan sat quietly contemplating his options, both hands, one on top of the other, on the pommel of his saddle. Gazing one way along the trail, and then the other. Finally, he said, "What do you think, Sergeant Major? That way?" He jerked his head, indicating the Trail to the southwest.

Coffin nodded his head and said, "Gotta be, Captain. He sure as hell didn't come all this way just to turn back."

"Let's go," O'Sullivan said, nudging Lightning's flanks with his spurs as he steered him onto the Trail.

Thirty minutes later, Beckler's Station came into view in the distance.

When they arrived at the station, it was a little after eleven o'clock in the morning. There was an Overland Mail stagecoach at the front of the store, and a dozen or more horses tied at the hitching rails outside various outbuilding, all of them except one bore military shabracks (saddle blankets) and saddles. There were also two Federal officers, a first and a second lieutenant, and a male civilian standing on the front porch of the store waiting for them.

"Captain," the more senior of the two officers said, and they both stood to attention and saluted. "Lieutenant Michael Roarke, 4th Kansas Cavalry; this is

Lieutenant Simms, and Mr. John Gordon; he's traveling with us to Fort Larned, and beyond."

"At ease, Lieutenant," O'Sullivan said, swinging himself down from Lightning's back and returning the salute. "I'm Captain O'Sullivan, 14th Kansas Cavalry. This is Lieutenant Warwick and Sergeant Major Coffin. It's good to see you. We need fresh horses and supplies, is the station manager available?"

Lieutenant Roarke, rather smaller than O'Sullivan, looked sadly up at him and said, "I'm afraid not, sir. Mr. Beckler, he's ... well, he's dead, sir, and everyone else too, including his wife. All of the horses and most of the supplies are gone."

"Holy Mary Mother o' God. What the hell happened?

"Comanches, sir. Three, maybe four days ago."

O'Sullivan turned his head and looked first at Coffin, then at Warwick, and finally Big Man. All three were looking stoically back at him; Coffin was very slowly shaking his head and frowning.

"What makes you think it was Comanche, Lieutenant?"

"Arrows, sir; they were are killed by arrows."

"Let me see 'em."

"Lieutenant," Roarke said and turned to Simms. Simms nodded, walked over to one of the horses at the hitching rail, then came back with three bloodstained arrows.

"We kept these, Captain," Simms said. "The rest we burned."

O'Sullivan examined them, first the steel tips, turning them over in his fingers, the feathers. There was a grim smile on his face when he handed them to the Osage scout.

"What do you make of 'em, Big Man?

"Comanche. See marks?" He indicated the colored bands just below the feathers.

"Me own thoughts exactly," O'Sullivan said, nodding his head, grimly.

"These not kill. Not go deep; not enough blood on shaft."

Roarke and Simms looked at the scout, aghast, then at O'Sullivan.

"If Comanches didn't kill them then who did?" Simms asked.

I'd say it was a gang of Confederate renegades we've been trailin' for more'n six hundred miles. Big Man, here, says we're not more'n four days behind em, but we lost track of 'em four miles, or so, back that way." he pointed with his right hand. "When did all this happen?"

"Three, four days ago," Roarke said, very quietly.

"Oh yes, it's them alright," O'Sullivan said, through his teeth. "Murderin' bastards, so they are."

"What did they leave, Lieutenant? Anything at all?"

"Not much, sir. We—my men and the stage—were slated to change horses, but they were all gone. We arrived two days ago, but we had to stay here and rest our animals so that they could continue. We're now two days behind schedule. We were just about ready to leave for Fort Larned when you arrived."

"Well, we won't keep you, Lieutenant. I assume you've looked after the folks."

"Yes, sir. We buried the bodies out back. I have not sent word either to Santa Fe or Fort Larned. Thought it would be best to keep my company intact, considering the Comanche, and all."

"You did right, Lieutenant. Though this wasn't Comanches. But there are plenty of Comanche that probably are keepin' an eye you. Better get movin', son. Folks at the fort need to know what's happened here, an' who did it. Don't want the wrong party catchin' the blame for somethin' they didn't do."

"Yes, sir." The two officers came attention and saluted. "We'll get the passengers on board and be on our way."

Fifteen minutes later, the four passengers, all male, were on board the coach, along with the driver and guard, and Mr. Gordon and the troopers were in the saddle, ready to leave.

"Good luck, Captain," Roarke said.

"Thank you, Lieutenant, an' the same to you. Keep your wits about you, you hear?"

Roarke smiled, nodded his head, and, with a wave of his hand, put spurs to horse and galloped after the coach.

O'Sullivan stood for a long moment and stared after them. Then, with his head bowed, he turned and walked slowly back to the store.

"Coffin, Lieutenant," he said. "We cain't stay here; it's too exposed, but we need supplies. See what you can find. There's a well over there. Have the men top up their canteens an' the casks."

He stepped up onto the front porch of the store and walked in through the front door, his boot heels thumping on the wooden boards sounded hollow in the empty building. He looked down at the stains on the floor, shook his head, walked through to the back: nothing. He stood for a moment, looking around, sniffing: something smelled bad. Then he shook his head and walked quickly out into the open air.

The men were at the well, drawing bucket after bucket of water; they did not see the cache of weapons at the bottom, hidden under a dozen feet of water.

"Big Man," O'Sullivan said, "how far are we from Las Vegas?"

The Osage thought for a moment, mentally calculating, then said, "Five days, no more, maybe less."

O'Sullivan nodded. Lieutenant Warwick, Sergeant Major Coffin, to me," he shouted.

Warwick came running around the store; Coffin came from the other direction, walking.

"Well, what did you find?" he asked.

They both looked at him, then shook their heads.

"As I thought, the son-of-a-bitch cleared everything out. Alright, there's not a thing we can do except keep on moving. We'll have to baby the animals for a while, till we can get to Las Vegas; five more days. In the meantime, we'll walk the horses for forty-five minutes, then rest 'em for fifteen.

"Which way did they go, Big Man?"

Less than a half-hour later they were mounted and following Quintana's trail westward toward the mountains.

Chapter 17

May 9, Las Vegas, New Mexico

O'Sullivan and his men arrived in Las Vegas late in the afternoon of May 9.

Quintana had passed by the wild frontier town three days earlier. He had stayed some three miles to the east of the town limits and had then turned due south, and headed toward El Paso, still three hundred miles away.

The two parties had more or less matched speed, but O'Sullivan's days had each been an hour, or more longer; the gap between them was now no more than sixty-five-miles, but O'Sullivan was in trouble; he needed fresh horses and supplies. Las Vegas was the place where he would be able to find both.

The livery stables were still open when they rode into town and that's where he made his first stop.

With the application of a little pressure on the stable owner, he traded the fourteen military mounts for fresh ones and the three pack mules for three more. He had to pay an extra fifteen dollars a head for each of the horses and ten dollars per mule, and he had to write a military promissory note for two hundred and fifty dollars more. And, as he was unwilling to give up Lightning and Coffin's mule, Phoebe, he bought two extra horses, one each for himself and the sergeant major. For these he had to pay what he considered an exorbitant two hundred dollars each. Even so, considering the good deal he'd received on the other seventeen animals, he wasn't too bothered, especially as they were both excellent mounts, healthy and strong.

He arranged to board all the animals overnight at the stable, and then went in search of a place to stay and something substantial to eat. He found both at the town's only two-story hotel. A bed for the night, dinner, and an early breakfast for all sixteen of them cost him another hundred and thirty dollars; Las Vegas was not only lawless, it was also expensive.

By eight-thirty the following morning, they were back in the saddle. O'Sullivan and Coffin riding their new mounts; Lightning and Phoebe were trailing along behind with the pack animals, both seemed more than a little perky because of their lack of a load.

O'Sullivan headed out into the desert, back the way they had come the day before, looking for the marker he had left the previous afternoon.

An hour later, they had found the marker and were again following Quintana's trail toward the Mexican border, three hundred miles away to the south; only ten days.

At eight-thirty the same morning, Quintana, was also getting under way. Now sure that he was beyond pursuit, he was in no great hurry.

Chapter 18

May 16, New Mexican Desert

The next six days passed by uneventfully, both for O'Sullivan and Quintana. By the morning of May 16, Quintana was within a hundred miles of El Paso and the Mexican border; O'Sullivan was less than a half-day behind him.

Quintana was still in no hurry, confident that he was not being pursued, and more intent on conserving his horses than maintaining a fast pace. As always, he posted scouts at the front and rear, each one maintaining his position a mile or so in front and behind the main group.

O'Sullivan, his troop bunched together in a column of twos, now had little trouble following the fresh signs on the desert floor—fresh hoof prints, fresh horse droppings, human waste—thus there was no longer any need for Big Man to range far ahead and he was now a part of the leading group comprised of the captain, Coffin, and Warwick.

At noon, O'Sullivan called a halt to rest, water, and feed the horses and pack animals. He was excited and nervous; all morning long, from just before dawn, they had maintained a steady trot, stopping for ten minutes every hour, as army regulations required. His quarry was now no more than ten miles ahead, and the hair on the back of his neck prickled at the thought.

O'Sullivan dismounted, dropped the reins, and walked on. He followed the signs for fifty yards, or so, then stopped, stood for a moment, and looked off into the distance at the silhouette of a low range of hills, which were not much more than a distant outline on the horizon that wavered and shimmered in the heat of the noonday sun.

Suddenly, caught unaware, he felt a not-too-gentle bunt in the center of his back.

"Whoa," he said, aloud, knowing that Lightning had followed him into the desert and was looking for attention.

"There he is, me old son," he whispered to the horse, he slid his right hand under the horse's neck and rubbed its cheek, affectionately.

"Not too much longer. Hang in there with me just a little while longer, and then we'll go home."

The great horse whickered, nodded his head, and swung it to the left, shoving O'Sullivan two steps sideways.

"Come on, old fella. Let's get that saddle off. I'll ride Dusty for the rest of the day; you can follow along an' take it easy." He undid the horse's leathers, took hold of the reins, and walked the horse back to the group. Ten minutes later, he had switched horses and they were heading toward the hills, following the signs Quintana had so obligingly left for them.

Quintana was indeed among the hills, and he too was stopping every hour, or so, not because of any army regulation, but simply to conserve his horses. He was, he knew, now slightly less than a hundred miles from El Paso, and that it was time to think about the route he intended to take across the border. El Paso itself was out of the question: too heavy a Federal military presence. He would either have to bypass the town to the east or to the west; he chose to go west, through the mountains, but first, he still had eighty of more miles of desert and low-lying hills to negotiate.

They were all seated on their saddles, the horses at rest, a small fire blazed under a large pot; the aroma of strong coffee wafting across the hills on a gentle easterly breeze.

Quintana looked around at the thirteen men seated around him—all that was left of his once fearsome company of cavalry. He shook his head, gloomily, thinking of glorious days gone by, of fast times, and heroic (in his eyes) deeds. He smiled to himself when he thought of Billy Quantrill, long dead now: *Now there was a man*, he thought. *A good soldier. They don't make 'em like that no more.*

He sighed, looked at his scruffy bunch, dirty, unkempt, unshaven. He stroked his own beard, took off his kepi, ran his fingers through his straggly hair and sighed again. *Damn, what wouldn't I give for a hot bath and a soft bed? Soon ... soon, just a few days more.* Then he smiled as he thought of the Mexican maidens that worked the saloons just over the border in Juarez.

He looked at them again, and snorted aloud. They all turned and looked at him. He shook his head, indicating he had nothing to say.

Christ, he thought, *what a sorry-looking bunch. What have I come down to?* He didn't respect his men at all. They were simply a means to an end, and he would discard them as soon as he no longer needed them. Again, he smiled at the thought.

"Saddle up," he shouted. "Let's get the hell outa heah. Gould, you go on ahead; Booger, you stay heah; give us an hour, then follow on. Heah, take these," he tossed the brass-bound binoculars that had once belonged to the dead Sergeant Brown to him, and said, "Keep a sharp lookout, y'heah?"

Booger Whitlock caught the glasses and smiled to himself. *Time for a nap,* he thought, but he didn't say so. And after all, they hadn't set eyes on a living soul for more than a week.

"You bet, Lieutenant."

Booger, knowing he had at least an hour to spare, didn't bother to saddle his horse. Instead, he remained seated and watched the rest of the group saddle up, mount, and then ride away to the south, picking their way among the rocks and juniper. Then he stood, picked up his saddle and the field glasses, and walked a few yards to where he had an unobstructed view over the desert to the north. There, he threw down his saddle, put the glasses to his eyes and swept them back and forth, east to west, several times: nothing. He grinned, sat down, leaned back, rested his head on his saddle and closed his eyes.

Not thirty minutes later, he awoke with a start; he had no idea why, but he was perturbed. He sat up, looked out over the desert: nothing ... then, *What the hell* ... three, maybe four miles away, a little more than midway between where he was siting and the horizon, he saw something moving. Something...

He stood, put the glasses to his eyes, stared through them and gasped. There in the distance was a troop of Federal cavalry, its guidon fluttering at the head of the column indicated that they were moving quite quickly.

He grabbed his saddle, ran to where his horse was tethered, threw it over its back, wrenched the leathers tight, and flung himself up onto his mount and galloped off after Quintana.

Down on the desert floor, unaware that he had been spotted, O'Sullivan and his troop were heading for the hills, now less than four miles away.

Booger Whitlock soon caught up with Quintana; they had travelled not much more than a mile. Quintana called a halt when he heard Whitlock's horse's steel-shod hooves clattering over the rocks. He turned, walked his horse back to the rear of the column, and waited.

In less than a minute, Whitlock rounded the bend at full gallop, whipping his horse with the reins.

"*What the hell?*" Quintana thought.

"Cavalry," Whitlock shouted, hauling his horse to a long skittering halt, its haunches so low they almost touched the ground. "Federal cavalry, in the desert."

Quintana immediately came alert. "How many? Where?" he snapped.

"Three, maybe four miles, coming fast."

"How many, dammit?"

"I counted sixteen, no more'n that."

Quintana visibly relaxed, and thought for a moment. *Well, cain't say I'm surprised. Only surprise is, it took 'em so long. So, only sixteen. That shouldn't be too difficult.*

He looked around at the surrounding hills. *Perfect!*

"Listen up," he shouted. "They're only sixteen, right, Booger?"

"Yessir!"

"So heah's what we're gonna do. No sense in runnin'. Best to pick our spot an' let 'em come to us. They think we don't know 'bout 'em, so we'll ride on, find the right spot, take cover, an' hit 'em hard. Move out."

They rode on for another thirty minutes, or so, until Quintana found what he was looking for. He passed through a series of rocky outcrops and defiles onto an open plain, strewn with large rocks, that undulated for several hundred yards to a point where the terrain rose sharply upward some fifty or sixty feet to a rocky ridge.

"That's it," Quintana said. "We'll get 'em when they're out in the open. Quick now, let's go."

They galloped across the plain, dodging the great rocks as they went and then scrambled up the steep slope. The horses were slipping and sliding as they tried to find purchase on the loose surface.

Once over the top, Quintana ordered the men to dismount. Ike and two more troopers were detailed to take care of the horses, the other nine men, Quintana ordered to spread themselves out along the top of the ridge and wait.

"Now listen up, you sons-o'-bitches," he yelled. "Don't none of you fire until I give the word, y'heah?" No one said a word but they all, including Quintana, hunkered down behind the rocks on top of the ridge to wait.

An hour later, with O'Sullivan leading and the Osage by his side, the men approached the gap between the rocks that gave access to the plain beyond. He still did not know that his column had been spotted and was more than a little surprised when Lightning stopped dead at the opening and refused to go any further. He nudged the horse's flanks with his spurs; the horse flinched, but didn't move. He tried again; the horse whinnied, but again didn't budge.

"Somethin's wrong," O'Sullivan said to the scout. "Back up," he said quietly to Warwick and Coffin who were just behind him. "Quietly, now!"

They moved back down the trail twenty yards or so, and O'Sullivan ordered the men to dismount. He turned Lightning over to one of the troopers, designated three more to look after the rest of the animals, and then the rest of them, O'Sullivan and Coffin leading, crept silently back toward the gap between the rock.

O'Sullivan, with his back against the rock at the right side, and Coffin and Warwick fifteen feet away with their backs to the rocks on the other side of the gap, peered through, searching for signs of movement. Nothing!

"You think Lightnin's just a bit spooky?" Coffin whispered across the gap.

"Spooky for sure, but not at nothin'. I'd trust that ol' boy with me life; just did. Somethin's up. Don't know what, but I trust that animal's instincts. Ain't the first time he's done this, an' he's never wrong."

Coffin and Warwick both nodded in agreement, though Warwick was not sure what they were talking about.

"I dunno," O'Sullivan whispered, more to himself that to the others.

"Coffin, you an' the rest stay back. See that rock over there?" He pointed to a large chunk of sandstone some thirty yards away in front and to the left. The gap between him and the rock was wide open.

Coffin nodded his head.

"I'm gonna make a try for it."

He put his head down, rocked back and forth on his feet a couple of times, then with a leap and a bound, he ran for the rock. He cleared the gap by no more than two strides, when a rifle shot rang out from on top of the ridge. He felt the wind of the ball as it screamed past his right ear. O'Sullivan slowed, swerved, turned, and dived back through the gap onto his belly, rolling and twisting, trying to make himself as small a target as possible.

"Holy Mary," he gasped, "that was bloody close, so it was."

For a moment, he lay there under cover of the overhanging rocks, then he twisted and rolled over onto his belly and levered himself to his feet.

"So, fella's, we have 'em. At least, they have us, for now anyway." He was smiling, seemingly in the best of moods, and why not? His quarry was close at hand, and he had just escaped death by no more than a couple of inches; the luck of the Irish was holding, at least for now.

"Back up down the trail, boys. We have some plannin' to do, so we have."

Four hundred and fifty yards away on top of the ridge, Quintana was beside himself with anger.

He walked, no he ran, pistol in hand, to where the trooper that had taken the shot at O'Sullivan now lay with his back against the rocks, cowing in fear of his commander's obvious wrath.

"You stupid son-of-a-bitch," he growled, in a low voice, cocking the Colt and pointing it at the trooper's head. "Didn't I tell you not to shoot until I gave the word? DIDN'T I?" He shook with anger, the gun trembling in his hand as his finger tightened on the trigger.

The face of the man on the floor went deathly white as he looked up past the muzzle of the gun into Quintana's steely eyes.

For a moment, Quintana seemed about to kill the cowering trooper, then he hesitated, took a deep breath, lowered the hammer, swung the weapon across his body and then back again. He whipped the end of the barrel across the man's face, inflicting a deep cut in his right cheek and breaking his nose.

"You'd best thank whatever God you pray to that I need every man I've got. If not, I would surely have sent you on your way, an' the same goes for the rest of you goddamn rats.

"Pay close attention to me," he growled. "If anythin' like this happens agin, I'll kill the man responsible. I'll not even think about it, not for a second. Y'heah?"

He turned away, walked a few steps to the rear, and threw himself down to think.

Damn an' blast it. Sheeit, sheeit, sheeit, sheeit! Stupid son-of-a-bitch. We had 'em, had 'em. Now what? Stay heah? Move on? Run? Cain't. Sheeit! He put his elbows on his knees, dropped his head into his hands, and sat there, his brain in a whirl; his men watching, silent, alarmed.

Finally, he seemed to jerk himself out of whatever strange world he had entered. He sat up straight, reached inside his coat, pulled out his battered pocket watch, flipped it open, noted the time, and looked up at the sun. *Four-thirty*, he thought. *Less than three hours till sundown. We'll wait 'em out. They cain't get outa that gap. We'll get outa heah after dark an' find a better spot, try agin.*

"Listen up, an' listen good," he said, quietly, grimly. "We'll wait till dark, then go. In the meantime, you keep them Henrys trained on that gap; anythin' moves, shoot it. Don't wait for me to tell ya; you do it. We gotta keep 'em holed up 'till we leave. Y'heah?"

They did.

O'Sullivan was also in a quandary: he knew that he couldn't move forward without taking serious casualties, and he couldn't go left or right, at least not in force, due to the terrain. There was nothing left for it but to go back and then try to circle around, either to the east or to the west, and that's what he decided to do.

"Lieutenant," he said to Warwick. "come here." He had his back to the rock on the left side of the gap. "They're there, up on that ridge," he indicated the direction with a nod of his head, trying to stay out of sight. "I'm gonna go back aways, see if I can get around 'em. I'll leave two men here with you. Put 'em up there, one on each side," he pointed upward at the top of the rocks on either side of the gap. "I need you to hold their attention, keep 'em busy. Sergeant Major," he said to Coffin, "you're with me. We'll leave the horses here and proceed on foot, this way."

O'Sullivan, Coffin, and the rest of the troop made their way back along the trail at the run, slipping and sliding on the loose surface as they went. For almost a half-mile they ran, until, at last, they were out of the hills and on flatter ground.

"Now then," O'Sullivan said, breathing heavily, and looking around. "This way." He turned to his left and headed west; behind them, they could hear the sounds of gunfire echoing among the hills.

For several hundred yards, they ran, skirting the rocks, then turned south again and back into the hills. O'Sullivan figured they were far enough to the west and on track to bring them up on the high ground above the ridge upon which Quintana was making his stand.

Quintana's men were keeping up a steady rate of fire across the plain, aiming at the white smoke on top of the bluffs on either side of the gap.

205

For all his rough edges, Quintana was an astute and intuitive tactician. One of the things that had enabled him to survive four years of guerilla warfare was his ability to put himself in his opponent's shoes, think like he would think: *What would I do, were it me down there?*

The answer was simple. *I'd back up an' circle around, try to gain the high ground.* He looked upward at the bluffs to his right and left, and smiled. *But which way? That's the question.* Again, he looked around him, made up his mind and nodded his head. *Ain't but two or three of 'em down there. They're already on the move,* he thought, looking over the ridge toward the gap.

"Hey, Booger, you Ike, Proust an' Gould; you stay heah. Keep their heads down. The rest of you, with me."

Quintana and the rest of his men scrambled south along the trail for about fifty yards until he found what he was looking for: a way up the slope onto the high ground to the west that would give him a view over the terrain. Whichever way they came, if they came, he would be able to spot them, and he would also be able to keep an eye on his men back down on the ridge.

The high ground upon which Quintana now deployed his men, was a vast expanse of rolling, undulating grasslands, strewn with rocks and boulders of varying sizes.

Quickly, he placed his men in a large semi-circle, with ten to fifteen feet between each one, and each man under cover of a rock, boulder, or natural depression. The emplacement offered a wide field of fire, ranging from east to west, with all three quadrants covered by at least two rifles. He found himself a spot, behind a low, flat rock, cocked his rifle, and settled down to wait.

For more than an hour they waited. Other than the sporadic gunfire from the gap and down on the ridge, there were no signs of life, but Quintana wasn't worried. He had what he considered the advantage, and he knew they must come from one direction or another, and he had all points covered. He pulled out his watch, flipped it open, looked at it, snapped it shut, and put it away—it was a little after five-thirty—the sun was low in the western sky.

"Won't be long, boys," he called in a low voice, barely loud enough for his men to hear. "Do not. I repeat, do not fire until I give the word."

Ten minutes more he waited. Then, out of the corner of his eye, he noticed something moving away to the west. It was no more than flash of light, the evening sun reflection of something metal.

Gotcha!

"Heah they come. To the west. Pick your targets, but don't fire until I say."

Quintana lay face down, his rifle resting on top of the rock behind which he had taken cover.

Another flash of light, then something moving, slowly, more movement, there, there ... there; blue, blue coats; closer now, ready...

"FIRE!"

The Henry rifle slammed back into his shoulder, nine more rifles exploded to his left and right. In the distance he watched as first one blue-coated figure, and then another, and another pitched over and fell.

"Whoopee! Hahaha!" Quintana yelled, laughing. "Give 'em hell, boys."

O'Sullivan and his men crested the rise and found themselves facing an undulating, open plain, open grassland, studded here and there with large rocks; the hills rising again, stark silhouettes against the evening sky.

He held up his hand, halting his men. He looked warily around. As far as he could see, under the darkening sky, there was nothing but waving grass, no signs of life. He nodded to himself, waved for his men to follow him and with his head down, bent almost double, he started slowly forward in the direction of the gunfire.

For several hundred yards they crept forward, O'Sullivan kept as many rocks between himself and the skyline as possible. Then, two hundred yards or more to the front, a single puff of white smoke followed immediately by: BAM! It was followed almost at once by a ripple of rifle fire and the shrill whine of the Minié balls.

To his right, one of his men pitched over backwards, hit high in the chest by the first shot, to his left, two more men fell in rapid succession.

"GET DOWN!" He yelled, diving flat on his face. "TAKE COVER!" He crawled quickly forward, his legs working frantically, like those of a frog, scrabbling and pushing, down into a small depression no more than two-feet deep.

Holy Mary Mother of God! The bastards were waitin' for us. Who and what the hell is this son-of-a-bitch? The who, he already knew; the what, he did not.

"KEEP YOUR HEADS DOWN! THEY HAVE US COVERED!"

He lay there for a moment and gathered his thoughts. He was shaken to the bone by the unexpected turn of events.

Oh this one is good, so he is. What now?" he thought, raising slowly to look over the edge of the depression.

BAM! The Minié ball whined past the top of his head, so close he felt the wind of it.

He ducked back down, rolled over onto his back, lowered the hammers of the Richards ten-gauge shot gun, looked right and left, and then crawled quickly to his left, along the bottom of the depression to where Coffin was also lying face down—his nose buried in the long grass.

"Goddamn it, Boone," he whispered. "The man's bloody psychic. How the hell did he know? An' what the hell is Warwick doin'? He's supposed to be keepin' their heads down."

209

"The man's nobody's fool, Captain. He knows what he's about."

"We lost three men, Boone, without even firin' a shot. Three! That's bloody terrible, so it is."

Very slowly, he raised his head to look over the top...

BAM! Wheeee. The ball passed only inches above his head.

"This is not good, Boone," he said, as he ducked down again.

He rolled over on his back, looked sideways over the top of Coffin's prone body, along the depression, and whispered, "There, see?"

Coffin looked. There was a large boulder maybe sixty yards farther along the depression to his left. He nodded.

"You go first," O'Sullivan whispered. "Stay flat. He has the high ground, so he can see every move."

Coffin crawled along the depression, flat on his belly, O'Sullivan followed right behind. Soon, they were behind the rock and in deep shadow; Coffin to the left, O'Sullivan to the right.

With extreme care, the two men raised themselves onto their knees, making sure to keep the great rock between them and the enemy.

They peered around the edge, inching their faces forward. Nothing. Then, O'Sullivan spotted something, slightly more than two hundred yards away: the profile of a head and part of the upper body of a man. He was behind a small boulder, rifle at his shoulder, looking out at the spot they had just left, but because of their new position O'Sullivan now had a clear shot. He looked at the Richards shotgun he was holding, shook his head, and whispered to Coffin. "Hey, gimme that Spencer. I got a shot at one of 'em. But this aint gonna make it." Here, he handed the shotgun to Coffin and took the rifle.

He checked the load; there was one in the chamber. Gently, to cause as little noise as possible, he pulled back the hammer with his thumb, then he sat for a moment, listening: nothing. He nodded, satisfied, peered around the edge of the rock; the man was still there.

Very slowly, making as little movement as possible, he raised the Spencer to his shoulder, sighted the weapon, and pulled the trigger.

BAM! The rifle slammed into his shoulder and, two hundred yards away, the Confederate soldier flipped over backward, killed instantly as the heavy .52 caliber ball smashed into the side of his head.

"YES!" O'Sullivan yelled, as he jacked another cartridge into the breach. As he did so, two hundred yards away, all hell broke loose as a ripple of gunfire from the nine remaining rifles opened up a continuous stream of fire on O'Sullivan's positions. Half-dozen balls splattered on the rock behind which the two men were hiding. They kept their heads down and waited. The rifle fire continued sporadically for several minutes more, then died away.

O'Sullivan lifted his head again, just in time to see a gray-clad figure running, head down toward the rear. He whipped the Spencer up to his shoulder and pulled the trigger.

BAM! The man cartwheeled face forward, pitched over once, then lay flat on his back, staring up at the sky, the blood pumping from a huge exit wound at the left side of his belly. O'Sullivan's shot had hit him in the lower back and passed straight through, tearing flesh, muscle, and intestines as it went. The man was dead in a matter of seconds.

For several minutes they lay under cover of the rock. The gunfire to the front and on the ridge had abated. O'Sullivan looked east and west, trying to spot his men. Nothing.

"THE 14TH! SOUND OFF!" He shouted.

"Here, here ... here, here ... He counted as they called in, ... *four, five ... Only five, plus me an' Boone ... we lost three. Damn.*

"AH'M HEAH, TOO, BLUE BELLY!" The voice echoed across the now almost pitch black grassland. "How you boys doin'? Not so good, huh?"

O'Sullivan turned his head and looked at Coffin: he was stunned.

"What?" he mouthed, silently.

Coffin merely shrugged his shoulders.

"YOU STILL THERE, BLUE BELLY? I knows y'are. Now lookee heah, I strongly suggest you boys pull outa heah. I has the high ground an' you're stymied ... that ain't the right word, now is it? Still, you get the ideah. You boys just pull on out an' we'll be on our way soonest, y'heah?"

O'Sullivan did not reply. Instead he peered around the rock, looking across the darkened grassland. He spotted something, something moving.

BAM!

"Oh come on now. You can do better'n that. It wasn't even close.

BAM!

The ball slammed into the side of the rock no more than three inches above O'Sullivan's head, showering him with shards of stone and dust.

"HOW'D I DO, YANKEE? BETTER KEEP Y'ALL'S HEADS DOWN. I'LL BLOW 'EM OFF IF YOU DON'T"

"Bejesus, that was close," he said aloud. "The bloody man can see in the dark."

"No, Captain, he up there watchin' for the muzzle flashes. He's one hell of a good shot. Better stay down. He's good enough to get you."

And so, they settled down to wait. Not another sound was heard from the enemy. An hour later, under cover of darkness, they crept back down the hill and rejoined Warwick.

"We'll need to wait until mornin'" O'Sullivan said. "We have men to bury."

"They'll be long gone by then, Captain," Warwick said.

"No matter. We ain't leavin' 'em for the vultures."

Chapter 19

May 18, New Mexican Desert

Quintana left the ridge under cover of darkness at around eight o'clock that evening, the 17th. He intended to travel through the night and put as much distance as possible between himself and the Federal cavalry, but the terrain made it impossible. The sky was overcast and the night was pitch black. For two hours they stumbled slowly through the darkness, until, at last, Quintana gave up and made camp.

He allowed no fire, and his men had little more than thin, threadbare blankets to keep out the cold of the desert night. By first light, they were on their feet, shivering and shaking from the cold. Now that daylight was upon them, Quintana allowed a fire and time enough only to feed the horses, make coffee, and warm themselves. By seven-o'clock they were back in the saddle and heading south. Due to the slow pace through the darkness the night before, they were no more than two miles ahead of O'Sullivan.

O'Sullivan also rose before dawn. As the first streaks of light appeared in the eastern sky, he had six of his men go and find the bodies of their three dead comrades. While they were quickly being buried under piles of rock, he ordered a fire built, breakfast cooked, and the animals fed and watered. A little after eight-thirty, now

215

satisfied that the bodies of his men were safe from scavengers, he order boots and saddles and resumed the chase. They were less than four miles behind him.

By nine o'clock, they had reached Quintana's now deserted camp. Big Man jumped down from his horse and went to the still smoldering campfire. He searched round the campfire and found a spot in the dirt where someone had thrown down the dregs from a mug of coffee. He stirred the spot with a forefinger, pinched a small amount between finger and thumb, raised it to his nose, sniffed, and threw it down. He searched again, found remains of a hard cracker, and a small piece of salt pork. He walked a few yards to the edge of the camp, found a place where someone had relived himself. He bent down, stirred the damp spot with a finger, sniffed it, then nodded and, wiping his hand on his britches, rose to his feet and walked back to his horse.

"Two hour, maybe three" he said, looking up at O'Sullivan. "No more."

"Alright," he said to the men gathered around him. "This man is no one's fool. He' knows he cain't outrun us, which means he has to stop us. If I were him, I'd want to do that the first chance I got. That bein' so, he's gonna be waitin' for us, somewhere. Somewhere close." He paused and thought for a moment.

"So," he continued, "here's what we'll do: Ross, Simpson," he said to two of the men. "You two are gonna stay back with the pack animals an' the spare horses. Stay back at least five hundred yards, and keep

216

'em safe. We get into trouble, we're gonna need 'em. You hear anythin' up ahead where we'll be, anythin' at all that sounds like a fight, you turn back, find some good cover, an' look after the animals and supplies. Y'hear?"

They did.

"That son-of-a-bitch," he said to the group in general, "will probably try to dismount us, same as he did the Comanche. The rest of us will move on, but, by God, keep your eyes peeled, an' when I give an order, you obey it immediately an' without thought. Big Man, you stay behind the lieutenant an' me. Do we all got it?"

"Yes sir," the answer rippled around the men.

O'Sullivan nodded, "Check your weapons. Keep 'em in your hands. Coffin, that mule needs to stay with Ross and Simpson, as does Lightin'. We'll ride the spares."

"Yes sir," Coffins said dismounting.

O'Sullivan also dismounted. They removed the saddles from the two mounts and transferred them to the two spare horses.

"Be safe, old fella," O'Sullivan whispered in the great horse's ear. Lightning nodded, nipped his shoulder, and whickered. O'Sullivan looked round at the smiling troopers, sheepishly, and said, "Yeh, yeh, yeh. Let's get movin'. No sense in givin' that bloody maniac any more time to prepare than need be."

He and Coffin remounted.

"Check your weapons, Boone."

O'Sullivan pulled the Richards from its scabbard, checked the loads, and returned it. He pulled first one Colt from its holster, checked it, replaced it, then the other. Finally, he pulled his horse's head around to face the proper direction, put spurs to its flanks, and trotted on.

Quintana was indeed no more than three hours ahead. In fact, the distance between the two groups was less than five miles, and he was worried, which was something new for him.

He was now sure he would not be able to outrun his pursuers, at least not without doing them some serious damage, and he also knew that he had to hit them sooner rather than later, and he had to hit them where they would not be expecting it.

He had just left one low range of hills and could see the outline of another about five, maybe six, miles farther on.

He halted the column, sat still in the saddle, looked to his left and right, and then again at the distant hills. *If I was him, that's where I would expect an ambush, up in those hills, so I needs to figure out somethin' different.*

He looked back at the undulating hills he had just left—maybe half a mile behind—and shook his head. *Cain't be more'n a couple hours behind. Got a goddamn savage with 'em, too, followin' me tracks. Cain't fool them sons-o'-bitches. They outa be outa the hills afore we can cross this godforsooken plain. Damn, damn, damn.*

He looked around some more, spotted something, and smiled, slyly.

Oh, yeh. Got it.

The plain was not really flat. In fact, it was a series of shallow swales and undulations—some of which ran parallel to the trail, some at various angles diagonal to the trail, and even more at right angles. Its surface was mostly rock, studded here and there with small boulders and rocky nodules. None of which would provide a whole lot of cover, but enough, at least, so Quintana figured.

"Follow me" he shouted, "an' stay close." He put spurs to horse and set off at a gallop toward the distant hills. For more than a mile, he and his men rode in a straight line at full gallop; then he called a halt, turned, and looked back at the hills from whence they'd come.

He pulled his glasses from the leather pouch on his saddle, put them to his eyes, and searched the hills for signs of life. Nothing.

Satisfied, he returned the glasses to their pouch, wheeled his horse to the left and galloped away at right angles to the trail. He continued on for another half-mile, and then, without breaking the horses' stride, made a long sweeping curve back toward the hills from which he had just come. A mile farther on, he was back almost at the point where he had started, but two hundred yards

219

farther on, and slightly more than three hundred yards to the left of the trail along which he expected his pursuers soon to appear.

He dismounted his troop, sent the horses to the rear in the charge of three of his men, and then deployed the rest of his men among the swales and depressions. Before he did so, however, he gathered them together and explained his plan.

"Them Yankees gonna come outa the hills, followin' our tracks. That savage is gonna lead 'em out along the trail past us heah. We let 'em get well past, then we hit 'em, out in the open, leavin' no chance for 'em to turn and head back for the hills.

"Hit the horses first, they're bigger targets, then get the troopers. If all goes well, we should be able to get 'em all before they knows what hit 'em."

And then he settled down to wait. It was a little after eleven-thirty in the morning, almost noon, and the sun was high in the sky. For more than an hour they waited, the heat of mid-day almost unbearable.

Quintana watched the trail through his glasses. For what seemed like hours, all was quiet, not even the insects seemed to be stirring, and then ... Quintana tensed, pressed the glasses hard against his eyes sockets. Something was moving.

"Get ready," he shouted in a low voice. Then, he squinted his eyes shut and gritted his teeth, fearing his voice would be heard. It wasn't. But, then...

"GODDAMMIT! FIRE!" Quintana screamed, throwing his glasses to the ground.

O'Sullivan, at the head of the troop, had an uneasy feeling that all was not well. He had halted them some hundred yards back along the trail and had walked slowly forward to a point where he could see out onto the plain. He stared all around, at the horizon and all points in between, but he could see nothing. Still, something, he felt deep in his bones, just wasn't right. He turned and, head down, walked back to where his men were waiting.

He remounted, sat still for several moments, thinking, then said, "Something's not right. Don't know what. I just know it; for one thing, it's too quiet."

He looked at Coffin, then at Warwick, "Maybe I'm goin' crazy, maybe. But, it don't matter. We ain't got nothin' to lose by bein' careful. Here's what I plan."

For several moments more he spoke—describing what he had in mind, and what each man's part would be. Then he walked his horse back to the front of the column. He stopped, sat for a moment, took several deep breaths, and then, he kicked the horse hard and yelled, "CHARGE!"

His horse reared under the shock of the spurs, then leaped forward and, with the rest of the troop trailing out behind him, he streaked along the trail and out onto the open plain.

As he hit open country, he heard a loud voice off to his left yell, "GODDAMNIT! FIRE!" And then it seemed like the world to his left had exploded.

He hadn't traveled more than a hundred yards when he felt the horse falter underneath him. As soon as he felt it, he pulled the horse's head sharply to the right and they careered on, away from the gunfire. He hadn't gone far when the horse began to snort uncontrollably, then it stumbled, staggered, and fell, throwing him headlong from the saddle.

He slammed down onto the hard surface, on his back, the air driven from his lungs. For a long moment, he lay there, breathing heavily forcing great gasps down into his lungs. Then, he lifted his head and looked around. Several riderless horses were galloping away from the gunfire. Several more lay dead.

It seemed that once again his intuition had saved him, and, at least some of his men, from destruction. He knew some were still alive because he could hear then returning fire.

Oh bejesus. Thank the Lord I had me wits about me.

"CEASE FIRE!" he shouted, rolling over onto his belly. Then, when the firing died down, he shouted, "Sound off." He listened as his men answered the call. *One, two ... Coffin, Warwick, come on, come on ... five, Big Man ... Seven, includin' me. That it? We lost five men? Five down, then. Holy Mary...*

"I MAKES THAT SEVEN, BLUE BELLY. Still think ya can get me? Hahahaha," again the insane laugh.

Son-of-a-bitch is tauntin' us. Don't answer.

"CAT GOT YOUR TONGUE, YANKEE?"

"Hey, Coffin, where you at?" He kept his voice low, trying not to give anything away to Quintana.

"Over here," came the whispered shout in return.

"Warwick?"

"Here."

"Get over here, crawl, keep your heads down, the rest of you men, you too."

One by one, they came crawling flat on their bellies, taking what cover they could from the undulations.

"This ain't good," he whispered. "That crazy son-of-a-bitch has us pinned down. We ain't gonna get outa this, less we figure somethin' out."

O'Sullivan took off his hat, slowly raised his head, and peered over the top of the swale. All was quiet, too quiet. He dropped down again.

"There ain't much cover. Me horse is just over there, an' there's another just there, to the right. They will provide some cover. But if we all stay here, it's just a matter of time before he wears us down. We somehow gotta take the offensive. Any ideas?"

"Can we get around behind 'em?" Coffin asked.

"Not that way," O'Sullivan said, pointing to the south, along the trail. "No cover at all that way. Maybe that way," he pointed back toward the hills from which they'd come. "It's about two hundred yards to the first real cover. Will take a while, but we don't have a whole lot of other options."

He looked at them each in turn, and then said, "Warwick, you go that way, keep your head down, take cover behind that horse," he pointed to the dead horse lying about twenty yards to the south, several yards on behind his own dead mount.

"Wait, wait, wait," he whispered, urgently, as Warwick began to move. "I ain't finished yet. When you get there, stay down an' keep an eye on me. Dammit, Warwick, I said to hold on; you'll get yourself killed."

Warwick rolled over onto his back, listened and waited.

"When I give the word, Sergeant Major, you get yourself behind my horse—not yet. Lieutenant, you take the other one. Rawlings," he gestured to one of the troopers, "you work your way over to the right. Big Man, you see if you can work your way to the rear, go as far as you can, until you're beyond their sightline. You two, you'll stay with me. When I give the word, you'll follow me, an' we'll head that way," he pointed, "back toward the hills, see if we cain't work our way around 'em.

"Now then, Warwick, Coffin, Rawlings, you head out, then when you get there, you keep your eyes on me. When I give the word, you fire in their direction. I wanna see what happens; see if we can draw their fire

224

and see where they are. An' then try to keep 'em busy, but don't take any chances. Go! Now!"

The three men wriggled off along the bottom of the swale. It took no more than a couple of minutes before they were in position.

O'Sullivan watched them go, waited until they were ready, slowly raised his hand, and then signaled for them to open fire.

BAM, BAM, BAM! They each jacked another shell into the breach and fired again.

BAM, BAM, BAM! Then they dropped back down, under cover of the dead horses.

The reply from Quintana's men was almost instantaneous. Four hundred yards away, eight Henry repeating rifles began a fusillade of fire that didn't stop, until Quintana, now almost apoplectic with rage, screamed for them to cease-fire. By the time the last round had been fired, they had expended more than a hundred and fifty shots; the two dead horses were peppered with Minié balls, not one of which hit the men hunkered down behind them.

Twenty yards away to the left, O'Sullivan had made a mental note of the positions of the muzzle flashes, and he grinned to himself. They were bunched together, closer than he thought, and they were a lot farther away from him than he had first believed. It was time to move,

----

To say that Quintana was angry that his men had fallen for such an obvious trick would be ... well, there was no describing exactly how angry he was. And O'Sullivan, while he was not quite right in thinking that Quintana was more than a little crazy, he certainly was not his usual, sharp-witted self. Whether it was the long days spent under the hot sun, the lack of decent food— much of what they had been eating these last few days was rancid deer meat—or simply the effects of four long years of war catching up with him, the man was certainly a little off, to say the least. Even so, he was just as cunning and conniving as he ever was.

Right now, he was boiling. He knew that his nemesis had his positions pinpointed, and he didn't like it. The trouble was, the positions he now held were ideal, easily defended, and he didn't want to leave them. Once again his intuitive mind took control. He sat back with his head resting against the rocks, his eyes closed, contemplating: *Now what would I do?* He thought. *He cain't stay there. It'll be dark in about three more hours, maybe a little more. His horses are gone. He's lost three men, down to nine in all. Not enough. He has to even the odds, but how? I need to hold out 'til dark.*

He rested, dozing, the rifles were quite, on both sides. He opened his eyes and sat up. *So, he cain't go south; it's wide open. He cain't come this way, we'd mow him down like corn. Only one way left to go...* He looked to the north, at the hills from which his pursuers had emerged only an hour, or so, ago, and he smiled.

It's gotta be that way; ain't no other choice, he thought. *So, by God, I'll just go meet him. Hahahaha. Ain't you in for a surprise, me Yankee friend.*

He gestured to three of his eight men to follow him. He told the other five to hold their present positions, and to keep the enemy busy and pinned down. And, then, followed by the three troopers—all of them keeping their heads well down—he headed east, to the rear, and down a long slope to the bottom of a small, grass valley. At the bottom of the slope, they turned and ran northward, along the valley floor, then turned west and began a long climb up into the hills.

O'Sullivan and his two troopers crawled on their bellies, for more than three hundred yards, almost to the point where they had burst out of the hills and into the open—the long crawl had taken them almost an hour, inching their way along on their bellies, to get there. They worked their way east for another three hundred yards, until he came to a point where he was sure that they were well to the north and rear of Quintana's positions; though the gap between him and them must now be at least four hundred yards.

From there, the three men, staying well under cover, clambered upward through the foothills onto the top of a low rise, staying on its north side, out of Quintana's line of sight. The excursion had taken almost two hours, their clothing filthy and torn, their knees and elbows—now exposed—were bleeding; open wounds caused by the constant contact with the rocky ground.

Gesturing for the two troopers to stay put and out of sight, O'Sullivan crept forward until he could see over the top of the rise. There they were—some of them, anyway. He could see at least five men in dirty gray uniforms lying on their bellies almost four hundred yards away, and perhaps fifty feet below his position. They were ensconced behind a natural barricade of limestone rocks.

Where the hell is Quintana, he thought, as he watched the five men. They were maintaining a slow rate of fire in the direction of where he had left Coffin, Warwick, and the others. Every now and again, one of his own men would return fire, the heavy balls from the Spencers shattering on the rock wall, showering the Confederate trooper with particles of stone and lead.

BAM ... BAM. Two more shots from the men below. O'Sullivan turned and beckoned his two men forward.

"Here, Spanno," he whispered. "Hand me that Spencer of yours. This shotgun ain't got the range. Stay down." He took the Spencer and handed the Richards over to him.

"Hoskins," he whispered to the other trooper, "you ease up here alongside me.

Hoskins crept forward and lay face down on O'Sullivan's left.

228

"Now, you see 'em?"

Hoskins nodded his head.

"Good. I'll take the farthest one, you take the closest; then I'll take the next farthest, an' you take the next nearest; we'll take the middle one together. You got that?

Again, Hoskins nodded his head.

"On my word, then ... wait ... Now!"

BAM, BAM! Two of the men behind the wall pitched upward and then fell backward. The other three, clearly startled, jerked backward away from the rocks and looked wildly around, trying to see where the shots had come from.

O'Sullivan and Hoskins cranked the levers of their Spencers and fired again.

BAM, BAM!

Another Confederate soldier flipped over backward, but, by now, the two remaining soldiers were on their feet and running.

"Damn, I missed him," O'Sullivan muttered, cranking the lever.

BAM, BAM! They both fired again; both Minié balls missed, but one of the two men tripped and fell, and tumbled onward, down the slope until finally he came to rest with his back against a large boulder. He scrambled to his feet, dodged behind the boulder, out of sight of the Federal cavalrymen on the hill, and joined his companion already under cover there.

"Three. We got three of 'em. How many does that leave, I wonder?" he said, more to himself than to his two companions. He peered over the top of the rise at the rock wall below: all was quiet. Then, a puff of white smoke to the left side of the boulder behind which the enemy troopers had disappeared, and BAM! Wheeee. SMACK. The Minié ball passed between O'Sullivan and Hoskins, and hit a large boulder just a few feet to the rear.

"Well, that one's still kickin', O'Sullivan said, "Where the hell are the rest of 'em?" As if in answer to his question: BAM! The heavy ball slammed into Hoskins as he lay flat on the north side of the rise. He had his arms in a forward position holding his rifle; the ball hit him under his left armpit and plowed on through between the ribs and into his heart. He died almost instantly, feeling only the heavy punch of the ball as it hammered into him.

O'Sullivan's reflexes kicked in, and he immediately rolled sideways down the slope to join Spanno, who was now lying on his belly facing the direction from whence the shot had seemed to come. O'Sullivan dropped flat alongside him.

"Cain't stay here," he whispered. Spanno nodded his head in agreement. O'Sullivan looked around, searching for a way out. Then he heard the rumble of falling rock.

"Goddamn!" a voice shouted.

"Quintana," O'Sullivan said. "Gimme that shotgun," he said, almost wrenching it out of Spanno's hand and at the same time handing him the Spencer. "Now, quick, this way," he shouted, scrambling over the rocks and up the slope to the north.

BAM, BAM, BAM. Three balls slammed into the dirt behind them as they scrambled over the top of a low ridge and into the defile beyond.

Quintana was headed north along the valley floor when he heard the shots that killed three of his men behind the rock wall—although he didn't know that was what had happened. What he did know, however, was that his enemy had just given away his position, and with that thought, came an evil grin.

So, me fine friend. There you are.

He held up a hand and signaled for his men to halt. He noted the puffs of gun smoke up on the rise, more than three hundred yards away to the northwest, pinpointing his enemy's positions exactly.

He smiled grimly to himself, waved for the three men to follow him, and ran at full speed along the valley; then, he turned left and ran up the grassy slope toward the rocky terrain. They reached the cover of the hillside, breathless, and threw themselves down to rest, and get their breath. Then, they scrambled onward, up among the rocks and boulders toward the top.

Quintana held up his hand, stopped for a moment to listen, and then waved his hand up and down for his men to stay low. He crept forward, slowly inching his way to his left, until, finally, he gained a clear view through a narrow gap between two large rocks.

Ah, there y'are.

No more than a hundred yards away, on the north facing slope of a rocky rise, were two blue-clad soldiers, both armed with rifles, and both peering over the top of the rise toward where he had left his men.

Quintana raised his rifle, aimed it through the gap, took a deep breath, exhaled slowly, and pulled the trigger.

BAM!

The Federal soldier nearest to him jerked once as the Minié ball ploughed into the side of his chest; the man dropped his rifle, and lay still. The other, like a scalded cat rolled over and over, down the slope and out of sight.

Hot damn. Quintana grinned, delighted. *One more, one less. Now he has only six. We'll get a couple more, an' then make tracks.*

"Come on. Charlie, you go that way. You two, with me, this way."

Charlie did as he was told, and heading due north up the slope. Quintana turned to the south, and stepped slowly in that direction as he continued to watch the rise to the west. He put his weight on a loose rock; it gave way under him and he slipped over sideways, flailing, his arms trying to maintain his balance, to no avail.

"Goddamn!" He yelled as he fell. He landed six feet below, his rifle clattering down the rocks after him.

For just a moment, he lay there winded, and then he scrambled quickly to his feet, grabbed his rifle, and looked wildly around: nothing.

He beckoned his men to join him and then, together, the three of them continued to work their way around the side of the hill to the south. Suddenly, he spotted something moving quickly up the hill about eighty yards away. He threw his rifle up to his shoulder and fired three shots in quick succession, to no effect; all of them missed.

Unfortunately for Quintana, O'Sullivan and Spanno had gained the high ground and were now lying in wait for them.

They didn't have to wait long. Spanno was flat on his belly on top of a small bluff, looking down toward where Quintana and his men were creeping through the rocks, but, although he could hear movement, he couldn't see them, not yet.

Several feet below Spanno, O'Sullivan was on his feet and to his right, peering around the side of the bluff; the big Richards shotgun in his hands, both hammers cocked and ready.

The first of Quintana's two men crept out from behind a rock, making his way slowly from one point of cover to the next. As soon as he appeared, O'Sullivan threw the shotgun to his shoulder and fired.

BAM.

The .44 caliber lead ball and six smaller buckshot slammed into the man's chest, hurled him over backward, and he tumbled head over heels several hundred feet down the hillside. Finally, he came to rest, broken and twisted, at the bottom of the hill.

As O'Sullivan fired, Spanno raised himself to one knee and brought his rifle to his shoulder. Before he could fire, however, BAM!

High up on the hill to the west, Quintana's man Charlie, had gained the summit and had fired down at Spanno. The ball hit Spanno on his right leg, tearing through the muscle and out again. Spanno flipped over and fell to the floor next to O'Sullivan, winded, and in excruciating pain.

O'Sullivan scrambled up and around him, spotted Charlie, who was already scrambling down the slope toward him.

He raised the shotgun, took careful aim, and pulled the second trigger. BAM!

It was a long shot for the shotgun, more than a hundred feet. The buckshot spread and missed by several feet; the .44 caliber ball, however, flew true, and hit Charlie high on the right side of his chest, spinning him around. His rifle flew from his grasp, his feet scrabbled on the loose shale, trying to keep his footing, but it was no good. His feet slipped out from under him, he slid sideways, tipped over, and fell more than twenty feet, and landed on his head, driving whatever life there was left, out of him.

Down below, among the rocks and boulders, Quintana saw Charlie cartwheel off the face of the hill, and he heard the crunch as he landed. Now, with the knowledge that he had just lost two more men, Quintana realized his position was probably untenable; his enemy held the high ground. He thought for a moment: he'd lost two for one, not knowing that Charlie had put Spanno out of the game, and then quickly decided that retreat was his best defense.

He signaled to the one man that was left to him, and, together they began working their way back the way they had come. It was several minutes before he regained the valley floor. Once there, the two men ran quickly back to where the horses were hidden.

Quintana checked to make sure the horses were safe, then ran to where his other two men were, now back at the rock wall and exchanging fire across the plain.

"Hey," he yelled when he was close enough for them to hear him. "Let's go. NOW!"

The two men turned and ran toward him, heads low, and rounded the boulder where they had not too long ago taken cover from O'Sullivan's fire from the hillside.

It was a little after four o'clock in the afternoon when Quintana and his six remaining men galloped south along the floor and then up onto the plain, heading for the low range of hills some four miles away.

Still high on the hillside, O'Sullivan watched them go, his lips pursed. Then, he shook his head, bent down, and lifted the wounded Spanno to his feet. He wrapped the man's arm around his shoulder, and together they stumbled down the hillside and across the grassland to where Coffin, Warwick, Big Man, and a badly wounded trooper Rawlings, were sitting with their backs leaning against the dead horses.

O'Sullivan eased the wounded Spanno to a comfortable sitting position against one of the dead horses and flopped down beside him. He looked around at the carnage, shook his head, took out his pocket watch, flipped it open, and noted the time. It was five o'clock; the battle had lasted for almost four hours.

[OS plus five + Spanno; Q plus 6]

Chapter 19

May 18, Evening, New Mexico Desert

O'Sullivan, tired and hungry, sent Big Man back down the trail to fetch Ross and Simpson, the pack animals, Coffin's mule, and O'Sullivan's horse Lightning.

When the Osage had left, O'Sullivan turned to Coffin and Warwick. "He has six men left," he began "seven if we include him. There are eight of us, including the scout, Ross and Simpson, and the two wounded men; although that one," he indicated Rawlings who was lying on his back, unconscious and bleeding profusely from a gut wound, "will be gone by mornin, I think.

That son-of-a-bitch did exactly as I expected, he killed or ran off our mounts. As of right now, we have my horse, your mule, Coffin, an' two pack mules. There are, will be by mornin', seven of us, that means we're short five mounts. I did see several that managed to get away. When the others get here with Lightnin', I'll go see if I can round some of 'em up."

The men and horses arrived thirty minutes later; the sun was low in the sky, but there was still enough light left for O'Sullivan to go after the horses.

He rode back just after dark with four horses in tow; they were still one short.

"Strip that pack mule. Spanno will have ride it. Light a fire. We'll wait till first light, bury our dead, and then get back after 'em.

"Yeh, Lieutenant," O'Sullivan said, with a smile, "I know. You think we should turn back, right?"

"Er, no sir. I was just wondering if a fire is a good idea. Mightn't it give away our position?"

"Very true, me old son. But, I don't think it matters. They were headin' south hell for leather, an' he's lost five of his men. He's gonna make a run for the border. We'll get after him as soon as we can in the mornin'. In the meantime, I need somethin' to eat an' some hot coffee, so let's get that fire started."

Chapter 20

May 20, Southern New Mexico West of El Paso

O'Sullivan and his now depleted troop did not get back on the trail until after ten o'clock in the morning of the 19th. It took then that long to find and care for the dead; Rawlings did, indeed die during the night.

They traveled south, following Quintana's trail all day, and most of the night. By noon on the 20th, they had passed through the hills, and over more than twenty miles of grasslands, to find themselves on the edge of a sheer cliff that dropped away almost three hundred feet to the flatlands below.

From the top of the bluff, the view over the great plain below, now more desert than grasslands, seemed to stretch endlessly away into the distance. The mountains, far away on the southwestern horizon, shimmered under the harsh, noonday sunshine. They were barely visible, all but obscured by the haze. It was a stark, barren landscape; the desert studded here and there with juniper and yucca trees, and a wide variety of cacti. The temperature was in the low nineties, and not a hint of a breeze stirred what little grass there was.

O'Sullivan, Coffin, and Warwick, still in the saddle, sat together on the rim. They were high above the desert, just a few feet from the edge of the precipice and a three-hundred foot drop, a vertical plunge to vast piles of jagged rocks—monoliths that had, over thousands of years, split away and fallen from the cliff face above.

Their mounts were restless; they stamped their feet in an effort to back away from the precipice, nervous because of their proximity to oblivion. The scout, the two remaining troopers, Ross and Simpson, the wounded Spanno, and the mule stayed well back, and watched and listened.

They were all tired—exhausted might be a better word—especially the horses. The pace of their travels over the past several weeks had been grueling. For more than a week, during which time they had fought two devastating battles and lost more than half their force, they had slept little—taking turns, in pairs, to keep watch during the hours of darkness, uneasy due to the ever-present threat of the seemingly second-sighted Confederate guerilla leader, Jesse Quintana. Now, their goal was in sight, literally.

As the three men sat still on horseback with their field glasses to their eyes, far away in the distance, at least ten miles, they could just make out the small cloud of dust raised by the fleeing Confederate raiders.

"If they make it to the Mexican border," O'Sullivan said, "we'll lose them. How far is it, do you think?" He said to Warwick.

Warwick shrugged his shoulders, and said. "Not sure, maybe forty, fifty miles at most."

"More like fifty!" Coffin said.

"How many miles to the border, Big Man," O'Sullivan shouted, not bothering to lower his glasses, or to turn and look at the scout.

"Fifty, fifty five."

Coffin smiled, and nodded his head.

"And the mountains?"

"Twenty, no more."

"How far ahead do you think they are, Captain?" Warwick asked, lowering his glasses to rest them on the pommel of his saddle. Warwick's, horse shuddered, snorted, and took a small step back, making as if to turn away. Warwick pulled him gently back into line with a tug on the reins.

O'Sullivan didn't answer immediately. Instead, he looked first to the left along the rim, then to the right, and seeming to make up his mind, he said, "Further than it looks: maybe ten miles, as the crow flies. But we ain't crows."

He turned in the saddle, his right hand flat on Lightning's rump.

"Which way did they go, Big Man?"

The scout didn't hesitate. He twisted a little in the saddle and pointed along the rim to the east.

O'Sullivan nodded in agreement.

"That's what I thought," he said. "We gotta go east, find a way down, before we can turn south an' follow 'em. Who knows how far?" It was a question more to himself that to the others. "It could be as much as a day's ride, but I don't think so. They found a way down," he nodded toward the tiny cloud of dust in the distance. "We will, too. Damn, they're so near, yet so bloody far, so they are."

They continued to sit there quietly for several more minutes, and then O'Sullivan seemed to snap out of his reverie.

He sighed a deep sigh, and with a gentle tug on the reins, he backed Lightning away from the edge of the precipice, turned, and walked him the few steps to the rear to join the scout and the two troopers. He dismounted, removed the saddle, saddle blanket, and saddlebags from the horse, delved inside one of the saddlebags and pulled forth a large, flat bottle and a piece of cloth, a strip torn from an old blanket. He unscrewed the top of the bottle, poured a measure of thick, green salve onto the cloth, and began to rub it into the sores on Lightning's back, sores caused by the constant rub of the leather over many long days on the trail.

"I'm sorry, old fella-me-lad," he said to the horse as he rubbed. "Not much longer, I hope, an' you can have a nice long rest."

Lightning nodded his head enthusiastically, whickered, swung his great head around, and gently nipped O'Sullivan's shoulder.

"Hey, easy with them teeth," he said laughing.

The great horse whickered again, the muscles on his back rippling in reaction to O'Sullivan's gentle kneading.

"We ain't got no choice; we gotta catch 'em before they reach the border," O'Sullivan said. "We sure enough can chase 'em into Mexico, but it would be better not to have to do so, right, Lieutenant?" he said with a grin.

Warwick, also tending to the sores on the back of his own horse, looked at O'Sullivan and smiled, but he said nothing.

"Boone," O'Sullivan said, standing on tip-toe to look at him over Lightning's back. "I've been thinkin', we gotta be movin' a little quicker if we're gonna catch 'em. We cain't do that draggin' the two mules an' Spanno, along with us. They're slow, too slow, an' that means someone's going to have to stay behind an' take care of 'em. So, me old friend, I've made up me mind; that it will be you; you'll follow on as best as you can."

"I can do that, Captain," Coffin said without rancor. He'd known O'Sullivan long enough to understand that his was the logical decision, and that he, Coffin, was the obvious choice to bring up the rear.

"Lieutenant, you an' me and them three," O'Sullivan said as he twitched his head in the direction of the scout and the two remaining troopers, "we'll rest here for an hour, then make the best speed we can. They know we're after 'em, but they cain't know how close behind we are. We have to hope they're ridin' easy."

He bent over his saddle, unhooked one of his two canteens, held it to his ear and shook it, listened, shook his head, and then unscrewed the cap. He lifted it to his lips and took a small sip. He swilled the water around inside his cheeks; tilted back his head, gargled, and then swallowed.

"How much water do we have left, Boone?" he asked.

Coffin looked back at the remaining pack mule, took mental inventory, and then said, "They have about a canteen and a half each." He pointed, indicating the scout and the two troopers. "I have a half and two full ones, an' there are six more on the mule, an' the cask is about half full. How 'bout you?"

"What's left in here," O'Sullivan shook his canteen, there was almost nothing left inside, "an' another full one. Warwick?"

"The same, Captain."

"All right. Only God knows when we'll find more water. We have to keep enough for the horses; they come first. Boone, we'll fill all of the canteens from what's left in the cask. Warwick an' me will take another canteen each. You boys can do the same," he nodded to the scout and the two troopers. "That will leave the sergeant major with an extra one an' whatever's left in the cask. Everyone, just go careful with it. As I said, the horses come first; got it?"

All five men nodded their agreement.

"From here on," O'Sullivan continued, "we travel light. Unload anythin' you're not gonna need, an' that means bedrolls, packs, and the like; anythin'. Keep your saddlebags—ammunition only in 'em, an' some crackers, an' some coffee, enough for two days—but leave everythin' else, an' check your weapons. Boone, you'll load the mules with the essentials, leave the rest here, an' then catch up with us when you can. Now, go to it."

All five men, with the exception of Coffin, began divesting themselves and their mounts of spare clothing, bedrolls, and personal equipment for which there would be no immediate need. That done, all of the water canteens were refilled, and the extra canteens transferred from the pack mule. The wooden cask now was less than a quarter full, a little more than three gallons.

They were soon finished, and, after a short rest, were back in the saddle, grim-faced, but ready for what they were sure was to come.

"Oh, yes. Gimme that rifle, Boone" O'Sullivan said, handing the shotgun to Coffin. "You take this instead. I'll not need it, 'least I hope not, an' the Spencer will, no doubt, serve me better."

The two men exchanged weapons, and then, when all appeared to be ready: "Let's go!" O'Sullivan shouted.

"Boone, you take it easy, now. Y'hear? Stay sharp, an' catch up with us as soon as you can." Then he touched Lightning's flanks lightly with his spurs, and was gone.

Boone Coffin watched as the five men rode east along the crest of the rim at an easy canter. Then, he turned and gave his attention to the mule that had served him so well for more than two years.

"So, Phoebe, my love," he said, affectionately slapping the side of the big mule's neck, "it's just you an' me, Trooper Spanno, an' old Lulu here," he said, indicating the pack mule, "leastwise for now."

The big gray animal snorted, enthusiastically nodded her head, and then slurped her tongue wetly over his face from bottom to top. "Ugh." Coffin smiled, and backed away, wiping his face on his sleeve.

He checked his own equipment, dumped several of the heavier items (including the paniers), checked to make sure everything was secure, and had a couple of words with the wounded man—who was holding up surprisingly well, despite the blood-soaked bandage on his leg. He was, after all, quite seriously under the influence of strong drink, supplied by the resourceful Sergeant Major Coffin.

Coffin remounted and gently touched his spurs to the mule's flanks and they set of in the same direction as their departed companions, but at a slightly more leisurely pace; Spanno was singing quietly to himself.

Chapter 21

May 20, Evening, Southern New Mexico

O'Sullivan kept up the grueling pace, a fast canter, for the next six hours, stopping for ten minutes every hour to rest and water the horses. They hadn't gone more than a half-mile from where they had left Coffin, when they found a narrow trail down to the desert floor and, by nightfall, they had covered more than twenty miles. They had crossed the great plain and were now in the foothills of the mountains. As far as they could see, both to the east and to the west, they stretched way into the distance. The cliffs, jagged peaks and bluffs, rifts, crags, and scarps, towered above them as they winded their way through the defiles and arroyos in the foothills.

All through the long afternoon, they had followed the trail of hoof prints left by Quintana's gang. Judging from the said hoof prints, O'Sullivan considered himself to be right: there were now only seven of them.

As darkness fell, they found themselves on a narrow, winding trail that led seemingly upward without end, and eastward, ever eastward. They were on foot now, and in single file, the horses picking their way delicately through loose rocks and stones that littered the trail.

As darkness began to fall, they arrived on a small, rocky plateau about mid-way up the mountain, and O'Sullivan called a halt.

He looked around, nodded his head in approval, and then said, "We'll rest here 'til sunup," O'Sullivan said. "Cain't see a thing up ahead anyway. Don't wanta fall down the bloody mountain, do we? No fires," O'Sullivan said. "Do not even light up a smoke. Y'hear?"

They tethered the horses to a nearby juniper tree, stripped them of their saddles, tended their sores, wiped and rubbed their flanks with pieces of old blankets, fed and watered them, then settled down as best they could to rest. But rest did not come easy.

After twenty minutes, or so, of lying on his back on the hard ground, O'Sullivan rose, stepped over to the edge of the plateau and stood, staring out over the plain below, and an uninterrupted, panoramic view to the east, west and north. To the south, at his back, the face of the escarpment rose into the night sky, towering above him, upward from the plateau, a sheer rock face, that ascended for perhaps another thousand feet.

The night was clear, the sky a deep purple, almost black, and might have been, but for a new moon, no more than a slim, silver crescent that cast an eerie glow over the mountain and desert. The sky itself was a vast, jeweled expanse of more than a million stars that twinkled overhead; the constellation of Orion, the hunter, dominated the vast reaches of the firmament just to the south. In an hour, maybe two, he would disappear beyond the mountaintop.

It was a shadowy world that surrounded him, alive with the sounds of the creatures of the night: the screech of an owl, the constant drone of a billion crickets and cicadas. Far away in the distance a coyote howled, its long mournful call echoing through the rifts and arroyos, to be answered almost at once by another, and then another.

O'Sullivan heard something moving behind him; he turned quickly, and began to rise. But it was only Warwick. He, too, was unable to sleep.

The lieutenant sat down on the rock and, together, they stared out over the vast open space.

"Over there, see?" O'Sullivan said, pointing. "It's them. See the glow of the fire? It's well hidden, but you can see the red glow on the rocks."

Warwick squinted his eyes in the gloom, drew in a sharp breath, and said, "I see it. We got 'em. How far, d'you think?

"Nah, we don't got 'em, not yet, but they ain't far, maybe a mile, a mile and a half; no more'n that."

"We should catch up with them tomorrow then?"

"Yep, maybe so, but we got a problem. We need water. The horses cain't go much further unless we get some. Go get Big Man. We'll see what he thinks."

Warwick nodded, rose to his feet, and walked the few yards to where the Osage was sound asleep beside his horse.

"Hey, wake up. Captain needs you."

The Indian rose quickly and smoothly to his feet and then joined O'Sullivan at the edge of the plateau.

"We need water, Big Man," he said, not turning around to look at him; instead, he continued to stare at the distant glow of the enemy campfire.

The Osage nodded.

"There is water," he said.

O'Sullivan looked sharply up at him.

"Where?"

"That way." He pointed back along the trail from which they'd come.

"We just came from there. Why in the name of the Holy Virgin didn't you say something?"

"You not ask," the Osage said quietly.

"I not ask? I not ask? What kind of a fool statement is that, begorrah?" He shook his head in wonderment. "To be sure, I'll never understand you people. You don't think like us, for sure you don't. How far to the water?

"Two hours ... maybe more."

O'Sullivan shook his head in frustration.

"Gad dammit. Well, there's nothin' else for it. We gotta have water." He thought for a moment, and then said, with a sigh, "Fine. As soon as it's light enough to see we'll head back. Oh, Holy Mother, please save us all."

It was still almost dark when they made ready to move out the next morning. The moon had set, and only a faint glow on the horizon to the east gave any indication that the sun was about to rise. Even so, there was just enough light for them to saddle the horses and lead them back along the trail, westward. The Osage scout was in the lead.

By daylight, they had traveled a little more than a mile back along the trail to a point where, to the left, there was a narrow opening between the rocks that no one had noticed the previous day.

Big Man pointed, indicating that this was the way they needed to go, and then he led his horse through the gap. Beyond the opening, they found themselves on an even narrower trail, a trail strew with large chunks of rock and loose stone. For another mile, the path twisted and turned, first between one rocky outcrop and then another, until, at last, they heard the sound of rushing water—a waterfall.

Moments later, they stumbled out of the rocks and onto the wide banks of a small mountain stream that tumbled down, several hundreds of feet from the top of the mountain. Before them, a cascade of clear, cool spring water that sparkled, glittered, and gurgled in the morning sunshine.

But the Osage had been wrong, a rarity. The journey from the plateau hadn't taken two hours, it had taken more than three and, by the time they had watered the horses and replenished their canteens, it was after nine-thirty in the morning. They had a lot of ground to make up.

Far away to the east, Quintana was having troubles of his own. The going on the mountain was rough and slow, and he too was almost out of water. He and his men were also on foot. Not because of the terrain, but because the horses were in such poor shape that they were unable to carry them. Quintana and his men were tired. Their horses, even more so, many had lost shoes, and their hooves were split and cracked so that they were barely able to put one foot in front of the other. Even so, by the time O'Sullivan was able to turn back up the mountain and resume the chase, they were more than eight miles ahead.

By one o'clock in the afternoon, O'Sullivan and his small group had passed the plateau where they had spent the night and were almost at the top of the mountain. As they crested a ridge some three thousand feet above the great plain to the north, the trail widened and leveled out, and they were again able to mount up and ride.

The surface of the trail was polished stone and the steel shoes of the horses slipped and slid on the smooth surface, so the pace was slow and careful, and it did not improve more than a little the farther they traveled.

By mid-afternoon, they had crested the mountaintop, or so they thought. But, no! In wonderment, they stared out over the ragged terrain that stretched endlessly away to the south toward the Mexican border less than ten miles away. It was a wild and desolate world of towering peaks and deep defiles, a high desert—stark and forbidding, the likes of which none of them had ever seen before. They stared out over it in awe, wondering if, perhaps, this might be the end of the road. It was indeed a formidable and seemingly impassible barrier.

They stopped for the obligatory ten minutes to rest and water the horses, taking stock of their surroundings, trying to figure out how far ahead Quintana and his men might be.

"They cain't be far," O'Sullivan mused, more to himself than to his companions. "An' they must be short on water."

Still astride Lightning, he took his glasses from the leather pouch attached to his saddle, put them to his eyes, adjusted the focus, and scanned the rocky world in front of him.

It was an endless stretch of peaks, arroyos, bluffs, plateaus and defiles; a wild and desolate wilderness that shimmered and wavered under the hot afternoon sun. Other than the faint whisper of the constant breeze that blew across the crags and headlands, all was quite. Overhead, a red tail hawk soared on the thermal, the tips of its wing and tail feathers fluttering slightly as it slowly circled, searching for its evening meal.

And then he saw it, not more than four hundred yards away, at the top of a high bluff, a small puff of white smoke. It was followed by the sharp crack of a rifle and then, maybe a second later, the sharp, wet slap of the .44 caliber Minié ball as it hit the Osage scout in the neck. It tore through flesh and bone, smashed through the vertebrae and severed his spinal cord.

The scout made not a sound. For a long moment he sat still, his head tilted to one side from lack of support, and then he simply toppled sideways out of the saddle, dead before he hit the ground.

Chapter 22

May 21, Southern New Mexican Mountains

"GET DOWN!" O'Sullivan shouted, leaping out of the saddle. The order was not necessary. Barely had the scout's body hit the rocks than they were all out of the saddle and seeking cover.

"HOW YOU LIKE THAT, BLUE BELLY? Not a bad shot from this distance, heh?" The shouted questions echoed and reverberated back and forth over the mountains.

On top of the distant bluff, O'Sullivan saw the glint of sunlight reflecting off something, field glasses, perhaps.

"Better turn yo'seffs aroun' and head back the way y'all came. On'y more o' the same waitin' for you heah."

"GIVE IT UP, QUINTANA! You ain't got a chance.

"The hell I ain't. It's you that ain't got no chance. We can lay heah pick y'all off one at a time. An' how d'you know my name anyways?"

There was another white puff of smoke on the top of the bluff, followed by the crack of the rifle, and then the sharp whine of the Minié ball as it passed just over the top of the large rock behind which O'Sullivan had taken cover.

"I have ya outnumbered, Blue Belly. Better get outa heah. I has the high groun', an' ya knows what that means."

O'Sullivan turned and ran, head down, back to the trail where Ross was holding the horses. As he did so, another Minié ball whined overhead and splattered off the rocks fifty yards on down the trail.

He reached up and drew the Spencer rifle from its scabbard on Lightning's saddle. He checked the load, cranked a cartridge into the breach, then reached into one of the saddlebags, scooped out several handfuls of .52 caliber cartridges, filled his cartridge box, and stuffed several handfuls more into his pockets. Then, bent almost double, he ran back to his chosen spot, peered over the ridge, rested the Spencer on top of the rocks, made a mental note of the breeze, sighted the rifle on the spot where the puff of smoke had appeared, and then gently squeezed the trigger. The rifle slammed back into his shoulder, and he jacked another shell into the breach. As he did so, he saw a small cloud of dust where the ball hit the rocks, just to the left of where he supposed Quintana must be hiding.

"You'll will have to do better'n that. An' you'd better not stick up your haid, 'cause we has the drop on ya. Hahahahaha!"

The insane laugh echoed through the canyons, and was followed by another white puff of smoke; again the Minié ball howled between the rocks and smacked against a large boulder just to O'Sullivan's right.

O'Sullivan rolled over onto his back, looked left and right at Warwick and the trooper, then said, "The bastard has us pinned down. Simpson, go tell Ross to find somewhere to tether the horses and then both of you get back here. Warwick, you go that way." He pointed to the left. "When Ross and Simpson get back, I'll have 'em stay here and keep 'em busy while I go that way." He waved the riffle barrel toward the right. "Yes?"

Warwick nodded and, head low, he ran into the rocks and disappeared.

But O'Sullivan was not the only one with that idea. Quintana was also on the move.

After just a few minutes, Ross came running back with Simpson following.

O'Sullivan outlined his plan to them, and then deployed them behind the rocks about ten feet apart. That done, he turned and ran to his right, his head down, the Spencer at the trail. Only a few yards farther on, he found himself running along a narrow trail that he could see meandered through the rifts and defiles, first to the east for more than a hundred yards, and then it turned sharply to the left and downward. The downward trend continued for twenty or so yards, and the trail headed back up again, winding its way slowly but inevitably toward the left.

O'Sullivan heard the crack of Warwick's rifle, at least he assumed it was Warwick's, some distance off to the left, followed by a distant yell.

He got one of 'em. O'Sullivan grinned at the thought, and then he scrambled over the rocks, trying to find a vantage point that would provide him with an overview of Quintana's position.

Warwick's shot was quickly followed by two more, but closer.

Ross and Simpson! He smiled, nodded his head, and scrambled quickly upward. His boots slipped and slid on the loose shale, his kept his head down, the Spencer in his right hand, and his remaining Cold Army in his left.

And then the rate of fire on both sides increased. The continuous crack of a dozen rifles echoed back and forth across the mountains. He stopped, listened ... *Six ... maybe seven of 'em,* he thought. *An' they do have the high ground; that's not good.* He ground his teeth, frowned, shook his head in frustration, and continued his upward climb. The face of the cliff was steep, the going loose and treacherous. Finally, he made it to the top of the escarpment and, on hands and knees, scrambled onto the crest of a small bluff, and lay face down on the southern slope of a large boulder. The gunfire, now to his north, was closer, and continued unabated.

He peered over the top of the boulder, but could see nothing but the clouds of white gun smoke rising above a ridge from what he figured must be the enemy positions—more than three hundred yards away. Three or four hundred yards farther on, he could see more smoke. *Warwick and the others,* he thought.

The Confederates were sandwiched between himself and Warwick, but there was no clear view of them, no clear shot.

He looked around, searching for a way to get farther around them, to find an unobstructed view of Quintana's positions. He spotted a small defile to his right that appeared to offer a route in the right direction.

For ten minutes more, he scrambled over the difficult terrain. He followed the defile, climbing over boulders, up steep rock faces and outcrops, clambering up one steep slope, and then slithering down again. He stumbled and almost fell as his feet slipped and slid on the loose shale along the way, until, at last, he found what he was looking for.

Some twenty feet above his head he could see what appeared to be a small plateau. He scrambled quickly upward, reached the top, and threw himself face down. He looked over the edge and glanced quickly around. There it was, a small hollow, just a few feet below, a well-protected vantage point behind three large boulders. Quietly, he slithered down into the depression, took cover behind the boulders, and peered through the gaps between them.

There you are, you son-of-a-bitch. He had a clear view of them. *Five!* he counted. *I can see five, but where is he? No matter. Five will do, for now, anyways.*

He lay on his belly, jacked a cartridge into the breach of the Spencer, took careful aim through the gap, and then squeezed the trigger: BAM. Three hundred and fifty yards away, the man nearest to him seemed to leap into the air and fall over backward.

One!

Without thinking, he operated the lever, and pulled the trigger. BAM! And again, BAM!

...two, three!

Three down. *Damn, cain't see 'em now.* The rest of them were gone, at least from his view. *Maybe two left, plus Quintana. Now who's outnumbered, you son-of-a—*

The gunfire from Warwick's positions continued. Crack! Wheeeee. O'Sullivan jerked backward as a Minié ball smacked into the gap between the rocks and ricocheted onward, showering him with tiny, razor-sharp shards.

Damn, that was close. Time to move.

Reluctantly, he squeezed through a gap in the rocks, scrambled back down the face of the bluff, and into the defile. He looked, first one way, and then the other, made up his mind, and then set off running back the way he had come.

Twenty minutes later, he had made it all the way back to the place behind the rocks where he had left Simpson and Ross; Ross was already dead, a hole in his face where his nose had been. Simpson was lying on his back, blood still pumping from a wound in his chest, he was dead—all but for the dying; his last moments were seeping away into the loose gravel.

To the east, Warwick's Sharps rifle was silent.

O'Sullivan shook his head in sorrow as he took a last look at the now expired Simpson, and then he headed east through along the defile, following the direction Warwick had taken earlier. He found him a few moments later, lying on top of a pile of boulders a hundred yards or so from where he had left the two dead troopers.

At the sound of O'Sullivan's approach, he turned over onto his back, brought his rifle to the ready, saw who it was, and then smiled and waved.

"Hey, Cap. I think we got 'em all," he shouted. But he was wrong.

Just as he said it, high on top of a ridge, maybe a hundred yards away to the rear, BAM.

They had not gotten them all. Quintana had somehow managed to work his way around them, first to the east, and then the north, and now, although they could not see him, he had an unobstructed view of both Warwick and O'Sullivan.

The Minié ball slammed into Warwick's left thigh, spinning him sideways, backwards, and down onto the defile some ten feet below. And he lay there, jammed between two rocks, twisted, and unable to move.

O'Sullivan, head down, ran to him. There was a nasty graze on his forehead where he had hit his head on the rock during his fall. He was still alive, but barely conscious.

"How ya doin' down there?" Quintana shouted.

261

BAM! SMACK! Wheeee... The Minié ball ricocheted off the face of the cliff, only inches from O'Sullivan's head.

BAM! SMACK! The Spencer spun out of his hand, its forestock shattered, and clattered onto rocks.

O'Sullivan pulled the Colt from its holster and cocked it, looked wildly around, but could see nothing; Quintana was nowhere in sight.

"Oh now come on. Waddaya think you're gonna do with that, huh?

BAM! SMACK! The ball hit the ground between O'Sullivan's feet.

"Now, I thinks it might be best if you dropped that pea shooter," the voice was low and mocking. "I has the drop on ya.

"DO IT. NOW!"

O'Sullivan dropped the Colt.

"Good, now step back. Go on farther. That's it, back, back to the trail."

O'Sullivan backed slowly away along the defile.

"Warwick," O'Sullivan whispered. "Keep still, stay quiet. I'll be back; quick as I can."

"Yuh done good, Blue Belly. Yuh ... Aweee ... sheeit!"

There was a sound of falling rocks, something sliding, and then: "Goddamn that hurt."

His weapons gone, O'Sullivan, now back on the trail, had no other option but to run. He looked wildly around, spotted a narrow crevice between two giant rocks, ran to it, and looked inside. There was light on the other side. He squeezed through the crevice and soon found himself on a narrow ledge that stretched away for perhaps fifty yards and then disappeared around the end of the cliff face. The drop from the ledge was at least a hundred feet, perhaps more.

How the hell did I get m'self into this predicament? he thought. *Better move on; sitting bloody duck. Gotta try to make it 'round the end.* With his face to the rock, he began to move slowly along the ledge.

"Hey, Blue Belly."

O'Sullivan turned, looked backward and upward and saw Quintana, a small figure standing, legs apart, high on top of a bluff a hundred yards, or so, away to the east; his rifle at his shoulder.

CRACK!

Instinctively, O'Sullivan ducked and dropped to the ground, and the Minié ball slammed into the rock at the side of his head, showering him with sharp splinters of stone and distorted lead.

"That was a close one." The taunting voice echoed among the rocks.

CRACK! Wheeee. Another ball whirred over his head, ricocheted off the cliff face, and screamed off into the void.

"You keep your haid down now, y'heah? Hahahaha. Whooeee!"

Holy Mother Mary, he's gone bloody mad!

"Where are ya, boy? Ah'm a commin' for ya."

Gotta distract him. He looked again at the top of the bluff, but Quintana was no longer there. He breathed a sigh of relief, pressed his back to the rocky face, and began to inch his way more quickly along the ledge. He finally made it around the corner and was relieved to find that the ledge had widened, and started to descend. O'Sullivan ran, fast, along the ledge, heading down the mountain.

BAM! SMACK! The Minié ball slammed into the rocky face of the cliff, just inches in front of his face.

BAM! SMACK! Another slammed into the rock face just behind him.

"Hey. Not so fast. Ah'm havin' trouble keepin up with ya."

The son-of-a-bitch is playin' with me.

SMACK! Another ball slammed into the rock in front of his face.

O'Sullivan staggered back several feet, lost his footing on the loose shale, and pitched backward off the ledge. As he fell, he twisted in the air, trying to land on his feet, but in doing so, his right shoulder hit an outcrop, flipping him over. Finally, he landed flat on his back among the jagged rocks, just to the side of the trail some twenty feet below. The back of his head slammed against the ground, and there he lay, unable to move; stunned and disoriented.

"Well, now," Quintana said, scrambling down over the rocks to where O'Sullivan lay, barely conscious, his left arm broken and folded underneath him. "Here y'are, an' takin' a nap, too. Don't that beat all?"

He stood over O'Sullivan and looked down at him, grinning. Then he squatted and sat on a rock beside him and said, conversationally, "Y'know, ya really are somethin' else. You know you done kilt all m'men? Just me left now. Why did ya have to do that? Why did you have to hunt me down like that? What did I ever do to you? Yeh, we wuz at war. Enemies, sure, but that's all over now; the war's over. Whut you do it for?"

O'Sullivan tried to raise himself up onto his right elbow, but he couldn't. The pain was unbearable; his shoulder was out of its socket. He lay back again, his head resting on the shale floor, and he looked up at the grinning Confederate leader.

He lifted his head, gritted his teeth as the pain coursed through his upper body, gasped aloud, and then with his teeth clamped together, he whispered, "Remember Elbow, you son-of-a-bitch?"

"Oh now come on. Ain't no need to call a feller names." He screwed up his eyes, stared up at the sky, then said, "Elbow? Elbow? Elbow?" And then his eyes lit up and he said, "Oh yeh, I remember; little town, close to Fort Scott. Why, what's that to you?"

265

"That was my sister you an' your men raped, you stinkin' sack-o'-shit, and the man you murdered was her husband." O'Sullivan struggled, tried to raise himself, but couldn't.

"That little pregnint girl was your sister? Well now, don't that beat all?" he said, dreamily, thinking back, remembering. "Nice little thing she was too, as I recall. Not much of a poke though; no 'thusiasm, no 'thusiasm at all. An' you know, I always did regret killin' that little girl, but ... well, ya knows how it is, bein' war, an' all."

"Yeh, well. She ain't dead."

"Do tell. Now I'm right pleased to heah 'bout that. Now you, on the other hand ... You *are* daid ... well, not right this minute, y'understand, but ya might as well be. Just need to finish you off, is all, but first—"

He stood, pulled the big Bowie knife from its scabbard, then sat down again. He looked O'Sullivan in the eye, and then tapped him on the forehead with the flat of the blade. O'Sullivan flinched, looked up at him, hawked, and spit in his eye.

"Oh my," Quintana said, wiping the spittle away with his sleeve. "What ya do that fur? That warn't a very gentlemanly thing to do, not very gentlemanly 'tall. I'm sure they didn't teach you that in officer school."

"Get on with it you crazy bastard."

"Oh I will; I will. You can bet you life on that ... hahaha, y'already did, though, didn't ya? But, first, I'm

266

gonna tell ya how it's gonna be," he said, conversationally.

"First, I'm gonna get me a little piece o' you, a soonavere, as you might say." He held the knife up in front of O'Sullivan's face, the flat of the blade toward him, the steel glittering in the sunshine.

"I'm gonna take your scalp. Then, I'm gonna kill ya, but slow, real, real slow. See, you gotta pay for what ya done to me, for killin' all my men.

"Y'know, when I left Elbow that day—seems like a long time ago, now—I had twenny-three men, m'self included. Now they're all gone. Oh you didn't get 'em all. Them damn Yankees at the fort got two; had to kill three more m'self, well Brown did; too badly wounded to travel. An' them dadblamed Comanches got a half-dozen, well ... five. An' then you come along and done fur the rest. Now there's just me, an'..." he looked at him, an evil grin on his face, "you."

He shook his head, sighed, stared off into space, then seemed to get a grip of himself and continued, "Y'ever heared of the death of a thousan' cuts, Captain?" He looked down at O'Sullivan, questioningly, tapping the flat of the knife on his own knee. He was waiting for an answer but he got none, so he shrugged, and continued, "It's a Chinee thing. They call it ling chi. I learned 'bout it in California, afore the war—there's a lot of Chinks in California; came to help build the railroad, so I heah."

He seemed to be rambling, his mind elsewhere, then he gathered himself again and continued, "It's a lotta fun, well ... for me anyways; not so much fun for you. I done it a few times before. Here's how it works," he said, waving the big knife in front of O'Sullivan's face. "I cuts little bits an' slices, non-vital bits an' pieces, off y'body. First, I'll take slices o' flesh off y'arms, legs an' chest, bein' real careful not to cut any big ol' veins—don't want ya bleedin' to death before I'm ready for you t'go, now do I? No sir, 'corse not. Now, then, as y'can imagine, all that takes a while, maybe two, three hours, or so. An' ohhhh my, does it ever hurt? Yessir, it surely does. Then, when there's no room to take any moah, by then, you'll be just a great big ol' lump o' raw meat. Then, I'll chop off y'han's an' feet, an' then I might finish y'off, cut your throat, or somethin' ... maybe, or maybe not. We'll see. Maybe I'll just leave you out heah to slowly bleed to death, bake a little in the sunshine. We'll see, but first I want your scalp, and I want you to see it."

Holding the big knife in his right hand, he stood, walked around behind O'Sullivan, squatted down again behind his head, reached forward with his left hand, grabbed O'Sullivan's forelock, and pulled his head back. He grinned as O'Sullivan struggled, and tried to twist his head from side to side.

"Now hold still or.you'll hurt yourself. Hahahaha," he cackled. "I'll be done in just a minute. Done this lots o' times; it's easy, you'll see."

He leaned forward over O'Sullivan's head, placed the edge of the knife at the hairline above his forehead, and grinned as a small trickle of blood ran down O'Sullivan's face.

"Ready? Here we go..."

BAM!

Quintana's right forearm, between elbow and hand, disappeared in a shower of shattered bone, flesh, and blood. His hand, with the knife still grasped in it, went spinning into the air to land several yards away among the rocks.

"Damn!" Quintana, said, dazed, as he stared wide-eyed at the stump where his arm had once been, and the blood gushing out from it.

"Bye, you son of a bitch," Coffin said.

He was perhaps a dozen yards away, just off the trail; the barrel of the ten-gauge Richards shotgun was still smoking.

He pulled the second trigger. BAM, and Quintana's head exploded.

"Holy Mary, but you cut that fine," O'Sullivan gasped, his head now resting on the dead Confederate leader's leg. "Where the hell have you been?"

"Hey, I got here, didn't I? That trail wasn't easy, especially with two mules an' a half-dead trooper in tow. Where are the rest?"

"Hah, just me an' Warwick left, an' he's in pretty poor shape, I fancy. He's back that way, somewhere. Ouch!" He gasped, as he tried to move his right hand.

"Hold on, Cap. Let take a look at that."

Gently he lifted the big man into sitting position.

"Oweee," O'Sullivan squeezed his eyes tight shut as his left arm fell from behind his back. "It's broken, I think."

"Sure looks like it, but hold on while I fix this," and then, without warning, he jerked O'Sullivan's right arm with his left hand and hit the back of his shoulder hard with the heel of his right. With a sickening, dull click, the shoulder slipped back into place; O'Sullivan almost passed out from the pain. For a moment, he was unable to breathe; then he gasped, looked at Coffin, and said, "You sick son-of-a-bitch."

Coffin grinned. "Hahaha. Now, let's get that other arm fixed. Can you stand? Nope, you're lucky," he said, gently feeling the bones of O'Sullivan's left arm. "No break, but the wrist is very swollen; you probably sprained it. We'll wrap it up when we get back to the trail. Let's go find the boy."

They found Warwick still among the rocks, but sitting up with his back to a large boulder. He looked up and grinned when he saw Coffin and O'Sullivan.

"Is it over?" he asked.

"Yes, son, it's over, thanks to Boone, here. He needs to take a look at that leg of yours."

270

Five minutes later, Coffin stood, looked down at Warwick, then at O'Sullivan, and said, "Ain't much we can do for you here. The ball's in too far for me to try an' dig out, but it ain't bleedin' too bad. We'll get you outa here, stop the bleeding and head for El Paso. There'll be a surgeon there."

O'Sullivan nodded, "El Paso's what ... fifteen, twenty miles?"

"Maybe not even that," Coffin said. "Can you help me get him on his feet?"

O'Sullivan shook his head, "No can do, Boone."

"It's just you an' me, then, son. Let's get you up an' outa there."

It was a struggle, but less than thirty minutes later they were back at the trail where Ross and Coffin had left the animals. Spanno was sitting on a rock, singing softly to himself.

Coffin covered the bodies of the two troopers with loose rocks. It wasn't much, but it was the best he could do; it would, he hoped keep them safe from scavengers.

It took all of the rest of the day, and part of the next, before they rode onto the dusty street of El Paso.

O'Sullivan, now almost fully recovered from his fall, went looking for the military representative. He found him, a Captain, seated behind a desk in a small office at the end of the main street.

O'Sullivan explained who he was, handed the captain his now sadly dilapidated orders, and then outlined the events of the past several weeks. The captain listened, without interrupting. When he was done, the captain leaned back in his chair and stared at him.

"That, Captain, was one hell of a story. Where are your men now?"

"My sergeant major has taken them both to the doctor down the street. I'm not sure what kind of state they'll be in when the doc's finished with 'em, but I have to get back to Fort Scott."

"Well, you can't travel alone. That would be suicide, and I can't provide you with men, there are not enough at my disposal, but there's a stage due in from Santa Fe on Sunday; it will have a cavalry escort. It will leave again for the return trip on Monday. I suggest you and your men, if they are able, ride with them. There will be another stage leaving from Santa Fe to Fort Larned, and from there, there will be another to Kansas City. It will be a long trip, but I see no other option."

"It leaves on Monday? Six days from now." O'Sullivan shook his head, frustrated. "Well, as you say, Captain. It's the only option, so Monday it is."

O'Sullivan shook the captain's hand, thanked him, and then walked out into the hot sunshine. He stood for a moment, stretched his arms upward, and arched his back. It felt good.

A hundred yards, or so, down the street, he spotted Coffin coming out of the doctor's office. He held up a hand, waved, and then walked along the wooden sidewalk to meet him.

"How are they?" he asked when they met.

"Spanno's lost his arm, well, most of it. The doc managed to get the ball out of Warwick's leg. There's not too much damage. Fortunately, the boy's tough and fit. The muscle stopped the ball, an' it did some damage to that, an' it will take some time for it to heal; he will be stiff for a while, but he'll be alright."

"How long before they can travel?"

"Warwick should be up an' about in a couple of days, but probably will not be able to ride, at least for a while. Spanno? I don't know; a week, maybe."

"There's a stage leaving for Santa Fe on Monday, in six days, with an escort of cavalry; we need to be goin' with them. If there's room, Warwick can ride in that for a while, Spanno too; if not..." He shrugged his shoulders.

O'Sullivan, Coffin, and Warwick rode into Fort Scott thirty-three days later, at two o'clock in the afternoon, on Saturday July 1, three months almost to the day after they had set out on their long chase. Spanno, unable to travel, had been left in El Paso.

273

Chapter 23

July 3rd, Fort Scott, Kansas

"Sir, I need to return to Nashville, to my regiment, the 51st. I promised Colonel Streight that as soon as this ... this ... thing was done, I would return and resume my command."

Richard nodded his head, and then replied, "The 51st Indiana Volunteer Infantry Regiment, and Colonel Streight, are presently in San Antonio..." Richard hesitated for a moment, and then continued. "Captain, I am afraid I have taken something of a liberty. When you arrived back here two days ago, I sent Colonel Streight a telegraph informing him of your arrival. Since then we have been communicating back and forth, mostly about your future. I have also been in touch with Washington..." Again, he hesitated, but continued, "Here's the thing, Captain ... No ... please let me finish. I have a lot to say to you, and when I've said it, you will have some decisions to make.

"First, Colonel Streight informs me that he will muster out of the army quite soon, probably within the next several weeks. He also informed me that as soon as replacements are available, the 51st will be decommissioned and sent back to Indiana. That being so, Colonel Streight has, with his commanding general's approval of course, released you from your obligations. You can go home, today, if you want to. No. Please, let me finish" he held up his hand as O'Sullivan was about to speak.

"Second, the Indian wars in the territories are escalating. Almost every Indian nation I can name is on the warpath: the Apache, Cheyenne, Comanche, Sioux, Kiawah, Arapaho, you name it. All of this means that things will soon be very busy around here, and among the outposts to the west. Captain, I need officers, good officers, experienced officers; I want you."

O'Sullivan looked at Coffin; he seemed uncomfortable, as was he.

"As I mentioned before," Richard continued, "I have been in touch with Washington." He reached over his desk and handed O'Sullivan a single sheet of paper, a telegraph.

"As you can see, your commission as captain of cavalry in the regular United States Army has been confirmed; you are no longer a volunteer; Sergeant Major Coffin's rank has also been confirmed. If you decide to accept your appointments," he said, looking first at O'Sullivan, then at Coffin, "you will be assigned to one of the frontier outposts."

Richard looked at each of them in turn. O'Sullivan sat still in his chair, staring down at the piece of paper; Coffin watched him, a slight smile on his face.

"You do not need to decide immediately. When was the last time you had leave, either of you?"

"Hah," O'Sullivan laughed as he looked up at Colonel Richard. "It's been so long I can't remember when; before Shiloh, that's for sure."

"Going on four years, then," Richard said, nodding his head. "In which case, I suggest you both take a couple of weeks; take a little time with your sister. You both could do with the rest, I'm sure."

O'Sullivan looked at Richard, thoughtfully, then nodded his head, stood, offered the colonel his hand across the desk, and said, "Two weeks it shall be, Colonel, and thank you, sir."

"Good. I'll see you back at nine o'clock on—" he looked at his calendar, and said, "shall we the 17th, then? And then we can go from there."

Seven days later, a little after noon, O'Sullivan and Coffin were seated together in rockers on the wooden sidewalk at the front of Powell's General Store in Elbow.

"So Boone, you've had time to think," O'Sullivan said. "What have you decided?"

"That, Iggy, depends on you," Coffin said with a grin.

"Oh you done it now." He leaned sideways in his chair, grinned, and punched Coffin hard on his right shoulder. "I warned you, so I did. No one ever calls me that. That's the first time and the last, you hear?"

Coffin ruefully rubbed his shoulder; the punch had been playful, but O'Sullivan was a big man, and it had jarred him.

"Now, Ronan ... awe hell, Captain. I ain't never gonna get used to callin' you that. An' hell, Bonnie calls you Iggy; why not me?"

"First, Bonnie is me sister. Second I hate the bloody name, Iggy an' Ignatius both. Now, back to my question: what have you decided?"

Coffin was silent for a moment then said, "I ain't got no home to go to; neither have you, as far as I know. I ain't goin' back to Indiana, no matter what. If you decide to take up your commission in the cavalry, I'll go with you. If not ... well, I guess I'll head west, maybe go to Texas, join the Rangers."

"Whew." O'Sullivan breathed a huge sigh, then said, "Coffin, me old son, we've been together a long time, been through many a tough situation together. You've always had me back. I don't know what I'd do if you were gone, so I don't. There's nothin' for me in Indiana either. Bonnie an' you, an' little Michael, are all the family I've got..." He rocked quietly for several moments, thinking; Coffin did likewise.

"Boone," he said, leaning forward, his elbows on his knees. "Let's go fight Indians. What do you think?"

Coffin nodded, rose to his feet, turned to face O'Sullivan, and, with a huge grin on his face, offered him his hand.

O'Sullivan stood, took Coffin's hand, gripped it hard, pulled him in to his chest, hugged him for a few seconds, released him, and said, "Let's go see Colonel Richard. Ain't no sense in hangin' around here gettin' fat when we could be gettin' to know our new command."

Thank you.

If you liked this book, I really would appreciate it if you would take just a minute write a brief review on Amazon (just a sentence will do). It really does help. If you have comments or questions, you can contact me by email at blair@blairhoward.com, and you can visit my website http://www.blairhoward.com to view my blog, and for a complete list of my books. So, I thank you for purchasing the book. I hope you enjoyed reading it as much as I did writing it. If so, you may also enjoy my novels of the Civil War:

Comanche
A Novel of the Old West

On a dark day in April 1865, only days after the Civil War had ended, a band of former Confederate guerillas slaughtered more than forty Comanches, most of them women and children. Thus began a six-month reign of terror along the Santa Fe Trail as Comanche chief, White Eagle, took his revenge. The U.S. Cavalry was assigned the task of tracking White Eagle and his warriors down. Lieutenant Colonel Ignatius O'Sullivan's orders were to either bring them in or kill them. O'Sullivan, with two companies of cavalry tracked the Comanches through the mountains for more than six weeks, until....

O'Sullivan took to the trail in July of 1865, and followed them into the mountains along the northern border of Comanche lands. Can he bring the wily chief and his well-armed warriors to bay? Can his soldiers fight the Comanche on their own ground?

You can grab your copy here on Amazon for just $3.99. It's free to read for Kindle Unlimited members. Here's the actual link: http://www.amazon.com/dp/B00XLX9OSC

The Mule Soldiers
A Novel of the American Civil War

On a balmy day in April 1863, Union Colonel Abel D. Streight, at the head of a brigade of Federal infantry, set out on a 220-mile ride to destroy the Western and Atlantic Railroad at Rome, Georgia. The most fascinating thing about the raid is that Streight's brigade of four infantry regiments, almost 1,800 soldiers, was mounted on mules, a huge problem in itself; few of his men had ever ridden a horse, let alone a mule. But, not only did Streight have almost 1,600 stubborn and wily animals to contend with, he soon found himself being relentlessly pursued by the inimitable Confederate cavalry commander, General Nathan Bedford Forrest.

The raid soon turned into a running battle between Streight's raiders and Forrest's cavalry. For Streight, it was a long and tortuous journey across Northern Alabama. For Forrest, it was one defeat after another at the hands of the very "able" Abel Streight—even though he, Forrest, had the advantage of home territory and the sympathy and aid of the local populace.

There are some wildly hilarious moments involving the mules and their new masters; or is it the other way around? There's plenty of action and suspense, and an unforgettable cast of characters, real and fictional, animal and human; some you will come to love, some ... not so much.

Streight's Raid took place at the same time as, and was loosely coordinated with, the more famous Grierson's Raid (the inspiration for the book, The Horse Soldiers by Harold Sinclair, and the movie of the same name starring John Wayne and William Holden). Although Streight was probably unaware of Grierson's Raid, it's certainly true that he caused a diversion that contributed to the success of Grierson's Raid, and much confusion among the Confederate pursuers of both raids.

They say that truth is stranger than fiction. This amazing story proves that point; for the end of the story is ... well, unbelievable.

The Mule Soldiers is the true story—fictionalized—of Colonel Abel Streight's Raid into Northern Alabama that took place from 19 April to 3 May 1863. It is an enthralling and bittersweet story that will stay with you long after you have finished reading it.

You can grab your copy on Amazon. It's free to read for Kindle Unlimited members. Here's the link: http://www.amazon.com/dp/B00R0AIA1O

Chickamauga
A Novel of the American Civil War

Just after first light on the morning of September 18, 1863, in the deep woods on the banks of Chickamauga Creek, a single brigade of Federal infantry stumbled into a full division of Confederate cavalry, and so began one of the bloodiest conflicts of the American Civil War.

Chickamauga is the true story—fictionalized—of that momentous conflict. For two days, the Confederate Army of Tennessee, under the command of General Braxton Bragg, and the Federal Army of the Cumberland led by Major General William Rosecrans, tore at one another during a battle that ebbed and flowed, favoring first one side and then the other. But, the Devil is in the details, and a single, inaccurate battlefield report led to a glorious Confederate charge and the total and devastating defeat of the Federal army. Chickamauga is the story of heroism, desperate deeds, and death and destruction on a scale which had never been seen before.

The story of the Battle of Chickamauga is told through the eyes of the Generals who planned the grand strategies, and the soldiers who fought, often hand-to-hand, one of the bloodiest conflicts in American History.

Chickamauga is the intense story of the young men—the everyday soldiers, who must fight, not only the enemy, but also their own fears and inner doubts to find the courage to face seemingly insurmountable odds. It's also the story of their superior officers, and the generals who control their fates—men who are determined to charge into Hell itself to achieve victory. You'll stand side-by-side with them as they contest one disordered, ear splitting, ground shaking battle after another.

The author weaves unbelievable, but true, tales of breakdowns in communication, insubordinate commanders, and strategies that falter and fail in the heat of total war. You'll learn of the iron bonds forged between friends and companions on the battlefield, and morals and ideals brought into question. You will become a part of a victory achieved through pure grit and dogged determination, split-second decisions, and total dedication to the cause. Chickamauga is the story of ordinary people in extraordinary times.

This 1863 battle—on the banks of Chickamauga Creek, the River of Death—cost the armies of both sides more than 37,000 casualties; it was the bloodiest two days of the entire Civil War.

You can grab your copy on Amazon. It's free to read for Kindle Unlimited members. Here's the link: http://www.amazon.com/dp/B00MBU78HK

A Little More Than Kin
A Short Story of the Supernatural

This short story of the supernatural came from an idea I had many years ago when I was wandering around a grand old house turned hotel on Jeykll Island on the coast of Georgia. To be honest, I was being nosy. I was where I shouldn't have been. Anyway, I went into one of the rooms. It was bare except for a single piece of furniture and an old wooden washstand with a porcelain bowl and jug thereon. Even though it was the middle of summer, it was cold in that room and I had a weird feeling that I was being watched. I stayed only a couple of minutes and then left. No, nothing happened but that experience did provide the inspiration for this story, A Little More Than Kin. You can grab your copy here on Amazon. It's free for Kindle Unlimited members.

Here's   the   actual   link:
www.amazon.com/gp/product/B00YSDG6B2